IN THE FIELD

"Terminal One, this is Gateway. Status report."

"All ports are in position, Gateway. We have Bennatti in sight. He's killed two more hostages since we arrived, but I don't think he knows we're here yet."

"Understood, Terminal One. Move on my signal. Gateway out."

Click.

"Terminal Two, this is Gateway. Status report."

"No one's dared the police line, Gateway, but the reporters are getting bolder."

"What about Gaal and Najarian?"

"No sign of them, Gateway. The story's still young, though. Could be another five minutes. Maybe as many as 20. I think we should move ahead. It won't matter how we look taking Bennatti down on TV if he kills all of his hostages before we do anything."

"Understood, Terminal Two. Start talking to the press. Make it look like something's happening."

"Roger, Gateway."

"Gateway out."

Click.

"Terminal Three, this is Gateway. Status report."

"I'm busy, Gateway."

"Report, Terminal Three."

"I'm getting flak, Gateway. What did you expect? This wasn't the best idea in the first—"

"Skip the editorial, Terminal Three. Give me your status."

"I'm doing my best, but I can't tie up the Team forever. Utopia isn't going to care that we beat them to the scene. They're still going to send in T2M soon. Bennatti's a Terat, after all. The publicity alone—"

"Delay Tomorrow dispatch another half an hour, Terminal Three. Then report back."

"Half an hour!? Gateway, are you cr—"

"Gateway out."

Click.

*   *   *

"How goes it, Luke?" Grayson Lorey said, setting a steaming mug of coffee down on the edge of his partner's desk. "Director Harris is on line."

Special Agent Lucas Barrows set his radio earpiece to Receive Only and took a few sips from the coffee mug Gray had brought him.

"Team One's moving in on Bennatti now," Barrows said. "He hasn't moved from lower Ninth."

"Hostages?"

"Seventeen," Barrows said.

"Is that total or..." Gray almost couldn't get the word out. "...left?"

"Left."

Gray frowned and stared into his coffee. The thought of losing hostages to a terrorist — especially a Terat terrorist — disturbed him more deeply than he liked to admit. Especially to Barrows.

"Any word on what he wants?"

Barrows shook his head. "He hasn't said. According to his psych profile, though, he won't want anything. He's been growing progressively more unstable for the last three months. It's the nova taint problem all over again."

"What about the wonder twins?"

"They haven't arrived yet. Eddings wants the operation to go ahead."

"What about the 'Topians?"

"T2M-Americas has got to have heard by now, but I activated Walker in Mexico City when the NYPD called us. He's trying to put a bad spin on the fact that we got to this story first. Make it look like T2M would just be dragging its feet while we did the real work. They're probably coming already anyway."

"How much time?"

"I told Walker to give us half an hour."

"You think they're going to scoop us?"

"Maybe," Barrows admitted. "Unless Cisco can take Bennatti down before T2M gets there."

"What are his chances?"

"Even. We authorized Cisco to use 'clipsidol, but he doesn't have much else that'll give him an edge. Bennatti's dangerous, but he's not thinking his actions through. He's sloppy."

Barrows smiled at his own pun, hoping to show his younger partner his confidence in Cisco's team's capability, but his eye twitched. If Gray noticed, he refrained from saying anything.

"That should be enough for Director Harris for the time being," Gray said instead.

"I'll have more for him when I check in with Cisco again."

"Sure," Gray said, standing back up to leave. "I'll keep Harris posted. Be right back."

***

"...now take you live to New York City, where Elton Roberts is live on the scene of this shocking subway tragedy. Elton?"

"Thank you, Rhona. This is Elton Roberts in New York City. You can see behind me the Ninth Avenue subway station entrance, where local Teragen supporter, Giuseppe 'Sloppy Joe' Bennatti, terrorized and took hostage an esti-

mated 30 commuters shuttling to the Culvert subway line earlier this morning.

"Here with me now is Agent Lewis Eddings of the Directive, the first to arrive on the scene. Agent Eddings, recap for our viewers, if you will, how this story unfolded."

"Elton, around zero-four-hundred this morning, our operatives discovered Mister Bennatti leaving his residence in the Blackburn Hotel and making his way into the city. Agents followed Bennatti to——"

"Excuse me, Agent Eddings. Is the Directive in the habit of spying on private citizens?"

"The Directive monitors active members of the Teragen against the potential threat of anti-baseline terrorism, Elton. We also monitor the mental stability of certain novas whom we consider to be at risk for extreme behavior. In this instance, our vigilance proved well founded.

"When the West End B subway line stopped at the upper level Ninth Avenue station, Mister Bennatti attacked the subway operator on the lower level and refused to let any of the passengers leave the forward subway car."

"As I understand, Agent Eddings, the Ninth Avenue station has been closed for a number of years. Why were the passengers changing trains there?"

"The tracks on the upper level of the West End line between Ninth and Ditmas are closed for repairs and track work. The transit authority keeps the lower level track at Ninth Avenue operational as a shuttle between those stations for that very eventuality."

"I see. And does the Directive suspect Teragen involvement in the damage to the other part of the subway?"

"I.... Not at this time, Elton."

"In your opinion, then, Agent Eddings, is this situation a coordinated act of Teragen terrorism?"

"That's always difficult to say, Elton, but this rampage appears to have no political element to it. Bennatti has not made any formal demands, nor has a representative of the Teragen made a statement. As far as we have been able to determine, Bennatti's actions are individually motivated. Beyond that, we can't say at this time."

"Are Directive agents engaged in negotiations with Sloppy Joe right now? Or are you waiting for Utopia's Team Tomorrow to arrive?"

"In situations like this, Elton, we can't wait around for Team Tomorrow personnel to arrive. Directive agents have already begun to converge on the subway car where Bennatti is holding his hostages. We expect to have Bennatti in custody very soon."

"And just how many Directive agents are involved in this situation?"

"... Excuse me, Elton. I've got to get back across the police line. Something's happening on the platform."

*　　　*　　　*

"Terminal One to Terminal Two. Good work, Agent. Keep that reporter hooked, but don't tell him anything else. My team's about to move."

The radio earpiece worn by Special Agent Alfred Cisco picked up his sub-vocalized transmission and carried it out

of the depths of the New York subway tunnel to Eddings.

"Stir the Blue and Whites, and make sure the police are holding back the press. We're moving. And alert me if Gaal or Najarian show up before next contact. If they come in, I don't want them surprising Bennatti or my team."

"*Affirmative. Terminal Two out.*"

Tapping a stud on his earpiece, Cisco switched channels to contact Special Agent Barrows back at C3I. He informed Barrows that Team One was ready to proceed. Barrows wished Cisco luck and signed off. Cisco switched channels again and sub-vocalized his orders to the rest of his team.

"Now is the time, gents," he mouthed silently. "Port Two, move onto the train and take stock of how many hostages are left. Port One, coordinate with Terminal Two to make sure no one comes down into the tunnels from either side. Port Four, wait for Two's report then move in to assist recovering the hostages. Port Five, get the eclipsidol grenades ready. Everybody else, train sights on Bennatti when he emerges from the train. If I give the signal, or if he attacks, launch the grenades and get down. There's no telling how he might react to the 'clipsidol. It could get really messy. Keep his attention diverted from Ports Two and Four. And don't let him back onto the train with the hostages."

One by one, the members of his team replied in the affirmative. He kept the channel open and stood up from his hiding place.

*　　　*　　　*

"The word's in from Harris," Gray said as he walked back into the control room and sat down in his chair.

"That was fast," Barrows said, finishing off the last of his coffee. "I just activated Cisco. We didn't want to wait for the wonder twins any longer. We'll have to hold the press conference afterward instead. No action shots this time."

"It's a shame," Gray said, looking at the computer screen in front of Barrows. The screen showed four independent images in four separate windows. Three displayed streaming video feeds from the fiber-optic cameras mounted in the team leaders' headset; one displayed a cycle of images from OpNews, CNN Online and VSNBC. Each image in that box showed the crowds of police, reporters and bystanders gathered around the Ninth Avenue subway entrance. The view from Team Two's leader's camera showed the same scene from his angle on the opposite side of the crowd. Directive Blue and Whites stood out in each crowd shot as well.

"What did Harris say?" Barrows asked.

"He wants Bennatti brought in unhurt," Gray said. "It would be good to have the twins show the agents resolving this peacefully all the way around. Even if Bennatti doesn't deserve it."

In Cisco's camera's section of Barrow's computer screen, Gray could see blood on the subway platform and all over the inside of the forward car.

"Unhurt?" Barrows asked, incredulous. "Completely unhurt?"

"That's what he said," Gray nodded. "Bennatti is a link to the Teragen and the Aberrants both. Harris believes Beta Division can get him to roll on both if we take him with the kid gloves on."

"I wish I'd known that sooner," Barrows said. "I wouldn't have sent Cisco in on point. If Harris wanted a negotiator, *I*

should have gone in."

"How's Cisco at improvising?" Gray asked.

"He's a little aggressive."

"How's his team equipped?"

Barrows shook his head. "Two team members are carrying shock-nets, one has a mox gun, and three are carrying eclipsidol gas grenades. That's it for non-lethal arms."

"This is going to get ugly," Gray said.

"Using 'clipsidol on a freak like this? Yeah, probably."

*　　　*　　　*

Cisco's earpiece went silent after his new orders came down from Barrows, and he stood dumbfounded. Special Agent Barrows' original plan to subdue Bennatti had been simple. Bennatti's eruption several years ago had gone wrong somehow, turning Bennatti into the monstrosity the media had dubbed "Sloppy Joe." Bennatti's flesh and bone had eaten itself away from the inside, leaving his insides nothing more than a loose mass of sloshing organs that Bennatti had to support with an artificial carbon-titanium endoskeleton. The only thing that kept Bennatti from physically falling apart was a biokinetic force field, and the result was a sight nothing less than monstrous. More so than even the average Terat.

Cisco had been assigned to the mission because his own eruption had given him the ability to disrupt the quantum powers of other novas. Should Bennatti prove an uncontrollable threat, and should lethal force be required, Cisco had been authorized to use his abilities against Bennatti's force field to whatever extent the situation called for. Failing that, he was to use the eclipsidol, which would knock both their quantum powers offline for a matter of minutes, allowing the rest of the cell to get the upper hand on Bennatti. Now, for some reason, the plans had changed, and Cisco had no idea how to proceed. After a moment's hesitation, however, he sub-vocalized new orders to his team members.

"All Ports, stand down," he told them, moving his lips just enough for the receiver to pick up, and no more. "New orders. Port Four, I want you back here keeping the target covered with the grenade launchers. Port Six and Port Two, I want you on top of the train with your shock-nets ready. All else, take aim with sonics only. Repeat, sonics only."

When the team assented to the new orders — with no little surprise — Cisco moved. Making no attempt to conceal himself, he strolled out onto the lower platform of the Ninth Avenue subway station, walking to within 10 feet of the crowded forward car. Terrified faces peered out at him from the windows, and he could just make out Bennatti shambling up and down the aisle, gesturing wildly and knocking a few of the hostages around at random, burning them with his repulsive "skin." Standing so close, Cisco could smell the blood that coated more than one of the car's windows from the inside. His every instinct told him that Bennatti didn't deserve any careful treatment, but orders were orders. He cleared his throat, straightened his blue beret and put his hands out at his sides in a non-threatening manner.

"Giuseppe Bennatti," he called loudly and clearly across the echoing platform. "This is Special Agent Alfred Cisco, speaking on behalf of the Directive. You are under arrest."

N!tertainment

N!terview

N! the news

N!sight

N!tre nous

N!ternet

N!tv

fun N! games

help!

awards

legal stuff

search

[   ]

find!

N contact us

Watcher Organization Declares Intent Before United Nations

N the news

The History of the Directive

ASSOCIATED PRESS
NEW YORK, NY —

Silence filled the United Nations Building Tuesday morning, following an announcement by Petr Ilyanovich, head of the Russian Confederation Federal Security Service. Unscheduled and unannounced, Ilyanovich addressed a meeting of the full General Assembly from the chair of the delegate from the Russian Confederation, introducing an international collective of intelligence and reconnaissance professionals to be known only as the Directive. Allied in this venture with the Russian Confederation are Japan, the United States and the United Kingdom, each contributing money and manpower to the effort.

When questioned as to the exact function of this new organization, Ilyanovich was vague, although he mentioned "a mutual need to monitor the international climate of the Nova Age." The Directive, he claims, will serve as an intelligence agency with direct jurisdiction over territory controlled by its member nations. The organization will also uphold the standard treaties of extradition those countries have with non-affiliated countries worldwide. According to Ilyanovich, agents of the Directive will have the authority to detain "suspects," and they will be authorized to carry weapons and use deadly force in extreme circumstances. Ilyanovich also announced the intention of the Directive to employ a limited staff of nova operatives in high-risk situations.

After the conclusion of the assembly, Ilyanovich could not be reached for comment, nor would the RusCon delegate, Sergei Breshlinov. Yasuke Taka of the Japanese delegation offered only, "The government of Japan stands behind Mr. Ilyanovich's statement." Dennis Learman, delegate from the United States, responded to Ilyanovich's declaration by saying, "The United States supports the goals of the Directive. The organization exists to keep pace with the unfolding nova situation, to see to the national interests of its four member nations and to monitor the influence of Project Utopia on global politics."

Responding on behalf of Project Utopia, nova hero and Team Tomorrow leader Caestus Pax said, "Currently, Project Utopia does not view the Directive as a threat. Mister Ilyanovich's declaration, though unexpected, does not alarm us. Of course, if they're going to be keeping an eye on us, it's only fair and expected that we'll be watching them right back. However, with greater concerns like our environmental clean-up program, our peacekeeping efforts in Western Africa, the terraforming project in Ethiopia and the construction of our new facility in Palestine pressing, this Directive is still a low priority."

Neither Vladimir Sierka nor President Andrei Srebrianski of the Russian Confederation have offered comment. British Prime Minister Blair could not be reached as of press time.

The Dawn

If the formation of the Directive can be attributed to any one figure, Andrei Srebrianski is that one. Srebrianski had moved up from a position in the Committee for State Security (KGB) before the collapse of the Soviet Union, to the Director of the Federal Security Service (FSB) in Russia. It was Srebrianski who advised Boris Yeltsin not to support the governmental coup that threatened Mikhail Gorbachev. When the government of the Soviet Union finally collapsed on its own, Srebrianski was instrumental in contacting the leaders of Belarus and the Ukraine, who then allied with Yeltsin to form the Commonwealth of Independent States.

After the 1992 election in the Commonwealth declared Boris Yeltsin president, Srebrianski formed a task force designed to ferret out corruption and graft in the fledgling government. He combined elements of the FSB, the intelligence division of the Russian military and a special sub-division of the Russian police force (SOBRE) that had been created years before in the battle against the Russian "mafya." He appointed Petr Ilyanovich, a young, heroic commander in the SOBRE force and former agent of the KGB, as the head of this new task force. This force was so effective that, within months of its inception, it uncovered a burgeoning conspiracy in the Russian Parliament. This conspiracy intended to oust President Yeltsin and replace him with Vice-President Aleksandr Rutskoi. Srebrianski reported Ilyanovich's findings to Yeltsin, forcing the conspirators to act earlier than they had planned. After a tense military standoff, Rutskoi was arrested, and Yeltsin named Srebrianski as his new Vice-President. When Yeltsin died in 1999, Srebrianski ascended to the Presidency and named Ilyanovich to the advisory position he had once occupied himself.

However, the Russian people found Srebrianski a weak choice of successor. The grief he showed at Yeltsin's funeral and in press conferences dealing with Yeltsin's death so undermined his public image that the people of the Commonwealth considered him too emotional to address the civic and economic problems that had not died with Yeltsin. States seceded from the Commonwealth or from deals they had made with each other until border lines on OpNet maps were as useless as the proprietary currency that each would-be independent nation printed. At last, the shuddering, stumbling Russian economy shrieked into a tailspin, causing a backlash that sent destructive waves through the entire world economy.

Within a month, the nascent Project Utopia had stepped in to offer damage control. Nova scientists decades ahead of their baseline counterparts worked tirelessly side-by-side with Russian economists, but they reached no solution. In June of that same year, many Utopian economists were transferred from the Eastern European crisis to deal with the effects of the same situation in Japan, and prospects for a solution in Russia grew increasingly slim. The World Bank finally threw up its hands and did the equivalent of quarantining Russia economically with an exchange-rate freeze until the rest of the world's economy stabilized. Eventually, Japan managed to claw its way out of its economic mire, by relying on the profit potential of nova abilities.

Srebrianski, however, refused to take that approach, claiming that to gamble the fate of his entire homeland (shattered by depression, political isolationism and civil unrest, though it was) on nova altruism was beyond foolish. Instead, he took it upon himself, his personal staff and the heads of the various governmental ministries to find a way out of the economic crisis themselves. Numerous doomed proposals and failed social programs attested to just how broad a spectrum of ideas the disheartened council came up with, and the lack of hope drove many of Srebrianski's closest friends and allies to suicide.

Srebrianski's own health began to deteriorate subtly, and all seemed hopeless until one August night in 2000. In a scene that was quickly conceptualized in made-for-television films and countless documentaries for all posterity, Minister of the Treasury, Vladimir Sierka, collapsed to the ground clutching his head after a tense shouting match with President Srebrianski himself. Some claimed that Sierka had grown so frustrated with Srebrianski that he had given himself a stroke. Others purported that Srebrianski had grown so frustrated with Sierka that the President had actually punched the Minister. Regardless, the other officials rushed to the fallen Minister to help him to his feet. However, when he stood, something about him had changed. The most obvious difference everyone noted was that the crow's feet and haggard black bags around the Minister's eyes had disappeared. Also, Sierka had suddenly started to smile.

"I've just thought of something we hadn't considered," Sierka is rumored to have said, just before laying out the most daring, innovative and brilliant economic and political venture ever to have emerged from the lips of a single human being. Within seven months, the Russian Confederation arose from the political and economic maelstrom that had been the Commonwealth of Independent States. Riding the wave of Sierka's victory over the "Moscow Crash" of 1999, Srebrianski was elected the Confederation's first president.

In the Shadow of Greatness

Upon the emergence of the Russian Confederation, President Srebrianski's health ended its slow arc of descent, but he never seemed to quite recover fully. Merely walking through news-media interviews with nothing more than the requisite diplomatic tact, Srebrianski praised the Minister's contributions to the betterment of the Confederation, then publicly counted himself and all of Russia blessed to have finally received deliverance in the form of Vladimir Sierka. Once he had made these statements, he would close the interviews, claiming to be busy or to feel unwell. Meanwhile, Sierka rocketed to public superstardom. He toured all of the Confederation states and many of the surrounding countries in a matter of weeks, pausing only long enough step out of his personal helicopter, give a rousing speech and wave and pose for media snapshots before jumping back into his helicopter and taking off. Much of the world's attention focused on the hardier, younger nova, and Srebrianski all but sequestered himself to the routine of his position. In fact, the Presidency had become little more than a common desk job.

At this point, Ilyanovich came to the President in private. The first thing he asked was to be made Vice-President, now that the hard times had settled somewhat. Srebrianski flatly refused this request, however, having already named a close personal friend of Minister Sierka named Ivan Semenov to that position. Confused but not deterred, Ilyanovich pressed on with the proposal he had come to make initially. He had been doing research and collecting reconnaissance data on the so-called "novas" whose coming had christened the century, and the information he had gathered on the subject had frightened him. Although novas only numbered around 2,000-2,500 across the entire world at that point, no one seemed capable of thinking of anything else. Novas were being hailed as the saviors of the world, and there were fewer of them than the total number of workers in the Russian paper industry. It was unthinkable, and yet, one need only plug into the OpNet to see the reality. One need only turn on the television or the radio, and within 30 seconds, the word "nova" would invariably come up. And now, one man — *by himself* — had saved the entire Russian Commonwealth from ruin in less time than it had taken Srebrianski to earn his first promotion in the KGB.

Furthermore, the organization called Project Utopia had insinuated itself so tightly among the layers of bureaucracy within the United Nations that no international initiative could take place without Utopia's oversight. Worse, Ilyanovich pointed out, was the fact that Project Utopia actually sought out novas in a seeming attempt to gain a monopoly on them. The Project claimed to have the best interests of the world at heart, but Ilyanovich did not trust even so open an accumulation of power. Someone, he claimed, needed to watch the novas and those who sought to utilize them. By collecting intelligence on the new forces that had emerged to shape the destiny of the world, the Confederation could be pre-

pared for whatever eventuality came to light as a result of the Nova Age.

Although he did not buy into his old friend's growing sense of paranoia, Srebrianski agreed that the nova situation was one he could no longer ignore. Calling on vestiges of power that he himself believed now existed only on paper, Srebrianski authorized Ilyanovich to reactivate the task force that had discovered the conspiracy in the Russian parliament during Yeltsin's Presidency and deploy its agents as he saw fit. Srebrianski then asked Ilyanovich for nothing more than periodic progress reports and an especial assurance that Minister Sierka would not be "brought into the loop," as it were. They both knew that the Minister would not remain ignorant of the initiative for long, but they decided not to approach the Minister with any more information than he asked for specifically. With those factors in mind, Srebrianski promised he would take care of funding and equipment and generate enough top-end interference to allow the agents operating under this directive to work in relative secrecy.

Talked down from his paranoia, Ilyanovich accepted the assignment proudly. Taking his cue from Srebrianski, he called this elite cadre of watchers the Directive.

The Directive Grows

After less than a year of operation, Ilyanovich came to the conclusion that the Russian Confederation could not support the worldwide goals of the Directive on its own. Facing leftover prejudice from the Cold War in the Americas, suspicion throughout Europe and close-minded isolationism in the Far East, Ilyanovich found the Directive's efforts thwarted at every turn. Half of the resources he spent on the Directive's behalf had to be diverted into avoiding the detection of other world governments. Without consulting Srebrianski right away, Ilyanovich decided to expand the Directive's scope in order to better enable it to carry out its goals. Although he was perhaps a bit more paranoid than the situation called for, Ilyanovich decided to make his case to the Prime Minister of the United Kingdom.

The United Kingdom

To his surprise, Ilyanovich found Great Britain remarkably amenable to the ideals of the young Directive. In the preceding years, the UK had pulled up most of its stakes on the continent and receded to deal with its affairs on the islands almost exclusively. In 1997, Hong Kong reverted to Chinese rule from British governance, and all reports indicated that Great Britain was glad to relinquish

the responsibility. As refugees flooded the region from all over southeast Asia, keeping the peace and enforcing the laws in Hong Kong had long since outstripped the area's viability as a trading port between the East and the West. The English washed their hands of Hong Kong, putting on a show of grumbling over the return of the Chinese to the area, then got on with their lives.

At the same time, negotiations between the English government and Sinn Fein leader Gerry Adams had drawn a balance between Great Britain and the Irish Republican Army on UK soil. While still dancing around the topic of Irish independence, the government of Great Britain relinquished much of its control over Northern and Southern Ireland in exchange for an official denouncement and initiative of prosecution against the militant wing of the Irish Republican Army by the government of Ireland. Gaining momentum from the 1994 cease-fire between the IRA and the British government, Adams and the Sinn Fein complied with Britain's set condition and created a task force within the Irish military designed to flush out and hunt down the terrorist activity of the still-dissident IRA. The task force called on similar existing forces in the British government for aid, and together, the two groups eradicated many of the more vocal and daring terrorist elements. Practically castrated by the internecine prosecution, the IRA devoured itself from the inside, and its leaders fled the island or went into hiding. Confident that the tactic had worked, Great Britain relaxed its rulership over Ireland and united its Northern and Southern halves into one domain again. In practice, England still holds the reins over the island, but the arrangement has mollified the Irish thus far.

This trend of isolationism continued into the year 2000, in the wake of the "Moscow Crash." While countries around the world scrambled to repair the damage the crash had caused, Great Britain directed its attention inward. Rather than form international economic blocs or work with neighboring countries to stabilize worldwide exchange rates, the United Kingdom decided to crack down internally. While the English economy took a serious hit, the government and citizenry locked their nation's doors, remained calm and weathered the storm with admirable aplomb. When the economic troubles ended and the UN ceased its rate freeze, thus leading to the formation of the European Union, the United Kingdom found itself self-sufficient enough to stand on its own. Unable to force its participation in the union, the United Nations left the UK to its own devices.

Regardless of Great Britain's seeming distaste for outside interference, Petr Ilyanovich approached Calvin Lathrop, the chairman of Great Britain's Intelligence and Security Committee. The committee oversaw the actions and expenditures of MI5, MI6 and the Government Communications

Headquarters, and Ilyanovich entertained hopes of winning Lathrop over to the cause of the Directive. Well-versed in the skill of the English at the intelligence and espionage game, Ilyanovich saw in Great Britain a valuable ally in achieving the Directive's goals. English intelligence and counterintelligence had proven invaluable to the Allied victory in World War II and in helping to curb the tide of international terrorism since then. Taking this information into account, Ilyanovich invited Lathrop and a handful of trusted agents to join the Directive in January, 2001.

After a quick consultation with his associates in Parliament, Lathrop returned a flat refusal to Ilyanovich's proposal. The tide of public opinion had shifted to such a degree that England was all but ready to build a wall around the islands of the United Kingdom. Where they had to rely on imported resources in the past, perhaps they would rely on the ingenuity and ability of native novas. When internal social conflict arose, the British Security Services (MI5) would deal with it without outside interference. The United Kingdom would sustain itself, thank you very much.

Ilyanovich, however, had done his homework, and he knew which buttons to push. He pointed out to Lathrop that the rise of the Nova Age would necessarily mean an end to any country's isolation, despite that country's every intention. Any nova arising from within Great Britain would draw media attention from around the globe, and what with Project Utopia working with the UN to establish itself as the number one nova-relations organization in the world, the day would soon come when no British nova-related initiative could go unobserved by the rest of the world. By the same token, Ilyanovich explained, the nature of nova power was such that each being was no longer restricted to the confines of just one country or continent. Even should England build a wall behind which it could keep to itself, most novas could either climb it, fly over it or knock it down, bringing the attention of the world with them. This argument, more than any, convinced Lathrop and the houses of Parliament to agree with Ilyanovich that they must maintain vigilance. However, the English government instructed Lathrop to make it clear to Ilyanovich that the arrangement in no way signified a political or economic alliance between the two countries. Parliament was well within its authority to pull all support and funding for the operations of the Directive if that body deemed it necessary. For all intents and purposes, England had joined the Directive for no other reason than to keep an eye on the ways in which novas would affect the sovereign interests of the United Kingdom. Where those effects proved detrimental to the UK, Lathrop would use information gathered by the Directive to see that said detriments were dealt with in the most expeditious and economical way possible. Otherwise, Great Britain would no longer support the enterprise.

Japan

Ilyanovich's first trick after seducing Lathrop to the Directive's cause was to convince both Lathrop and President Srebrianski that the further recruitment of like-minded national governments was vital to the success of the Directive. It took money to decide which nation to invite, to figure out whom to approach within that nation and to unearth enough specific information on how novas would impact that nation's future. However, Srebrianski had not earmarked any resources for that specific purpose. Ever a cunning manipulator, Petr Ilyanovich introduced Calvin Lathrop to Andrei Srebrianski and made his case for the expansion of the Directive to include other national interests. With a bold, dynamic speech and strategically vague uses of the phrase "we think it would be best if...", Ilyanovich gave both men the impression that he and the other listener were already in agreement on his proposal. Either convinced of the soundness of his plan or simply convinced that they were outvoted, both Srebrianski and Lathrop went along with Ilyanovich's idea and agreed to devote resources to the inclusion of other countries into their burgeoning collective.

Wasting no time, Ilyanovich and Lathrop decided to approach Mitsu Nakamura, chairperson of the Finance Committee of the Diet. Nakamura also served on the Justice Committee and the Foreign Affairs Committee. Each of these qualifications made Nakamura seem an even more ideal choice to Lathrop and Ilyanovich. When their investigations revealed that Ms. Nakamura was also on warm terms with certain higher-ups in Kuro-Tek, her potential value to the Directive became inestimable. Reasoning that the best approach to take with Ms. Nakamura would be a straightforward one, the two men brought the proposal to her much like a business proposition. It took very little observation to see that the Japanese viewed novas as the saviors of their economy, rather than with the suspicion and guarded skepticism that had taken hold of Ilyanovich and Lathrop. The Japanese *Saisho* program had seen to that.

Initiated out of desperation, the program sought to subsidize the work of Japanese novas, in hopes that their work would prove profitable for Japan. Considering the fact that the "Moscow Crash" and the resulting economic turmoil had all but wiped out the Tokyo Stock Exchange, the Japanese government was all too eager to accept any program with an iota of merit. Although risky in its execution, the program saw immediate results. In mere months, Japan's technological industries had already begun a slow ascent back to the place of prominence it had once occupied. Kuro-Tek was at the forefront of that movement, leading the way with black-market technology that accounted for a sizeable fraction of Japan's GDP.

Therefore, well aware that any Japanese government official would have trouble seeing the rise of novas as a foreboding omen, Ilyanovich and Lathrop pitched the Directive with a much less suspicious spin. They chose to contact Nakamura with a proposal more in line with the Japanese national conscience. Pointing to novas as the most valuable commodity of the new age, they portrayed the Directive as an organization designed to protect its member nations' investment in these valuable individuals. Although making no secret of their own motives behind supporting the Directive, Ilyanovich and Lathrop demonstrated to Nakamura that if Japan failed to support the Directive as well, it would be missing out on an opportunity of unfathomable significance. By monitoring the activities of novas around the world, the Directive would gather what amounted to insider-trading information on the invaluable resources the novas represented. (They reasoned that having this information would give the member nations an economic and strategic advantage over novas, which would make the nations better able to manipulate the novas' efforts.) Nakamura was know fool; glad of the opportunity to be part of the driving force behind the political and economic influence of novas upon whom so much of Japan's economic future now rested, she garnered the approval of her country's government and (at the absolute insistence of its foremost blacktech manufacturer) joined the Directive as its representative.

The United States

Contrary to the expectation of the nascent Directive's leading representatives, the United States was perhaps the easiest "sell" of the Directive's formation. Long used to its position as "global policeman," the United States initially welcomed the introduction of Project Utopia. Arising from the dreams of an American philanthropist under the aegis of the Aeon Society and led by an American and former member of the Coast Guard, Project Utopia seemed the perfect expression of the American dream. A global older-brother figure who guided the nations of the world to a unified view of peace and prosperity was just the role America had taken in world affairs in decades past, and now, Project Utopia sought to fill that role itself. Taking on what seemed a decidedly American flavor in its earliest days, Utopia arose proclaiming its dedication to peace and prosperity for all mankind under one banner. The American media heaped acclaim on Project Utopia, and the first Utopian complexes were built on American soil.

However, not all voices in the American government were so welcoming and generous. Assistant Secretary of Defense, Elliot Stinson, resented Project Utopia's immediate coup on the world stage. Selected for the position in early 2001, Stinson had a reputation for never trusting any international initiative until he had examined it, played with it in his mind and picked it apart to his satisfaction. He was believed to be something of a close-minded, prejudiced, nationalistic bastard, which some people claimed was the reason President Schroer had not appointed him to the actual Secretary of Defense position outright. However, President Schroer and those who knew Stinson well knew that what most people mistook for iron-minded bias was just the expression of Stinson's thoroughness and unwillingness to let any outside influence affect his country adversely. The decision to appoint Lewis Huxley to the Cabinet was a political one with which Stinson wholeheartedly agreed.

As Utopia's influence grew, Stinson observed the ease with which it won over the American populace, and this worried him. He saw the ardor with which people beheld Team Tomorrow, and he feared for the sovereignty of his country's government. He did not make the mistake of thinking of Project Utopia as a distinctly American organization, as many American citizens and government officials did. He saw Utopia for the self-motivated, wholly independent operator that it was. He saw Team Tomorrow as a privately funded army of novas with loyalty to Utopia alone.

As for novas in general, Stinson reserved judgment. He recognized in them the potential for great gain and uncountable tragedy, but he acknowledged that the eventual part novas would play in history was in no way preordained. Stinson knew that novas would affect the world in proportion to how the world affected them. The proper influence on nova affairs, Stinson reasoned, would lead to the most amicable outcome between novas and baselines in the long run. He was not convinced, however, that Project Utopia represented that proper influence.

Ilyanovich discovered this hesitation on the part of Stinson to embrace Project Utopia through transcripts of Congressional hearings at which he testified, as well as misappropriated copies of more personal correspondence. Given this information, Ilyanovich knew how best to take on Stinson. He prepared countless arguments and proofs against Stinson's anticipated refusal to join any multinational operation that valued global progress above national interest. He created theoretical projections of Utopia's growing power and influence on world affairs, laying out the best and worst outcomes of a Utopia left to grow unchecked. Finally, Ilyanovich, Lathrop and Nakamura wrote up a draft of each member country's responsibilities and areas of specific concern, as well as extrapolating America's place in the organization. This report, known as the "Sternych Missive," became the defining statement of policy for the Directive. When they had finished the missive, they sent it to Stinson and invited him to join them for a meeting in Moscow.

And yet, some would say that Ilyanovich and the others need not have bothered with so much work. When Stinson received the Sternych Missive at his Pentagon office with the compiled report, he inspected it only cursorily, preferring to interview the visitors and examine the merit of their proposal personally. At the meeting in Moscow, he discussed with the others exactly what part the Directive would play in world affairs as said affairs related to novas. Furthermore, they discussed how they would either compete or cooperate with Project Utopia, hopefully acting as a check against it getting out of hand, but at least keeping an eye on it as a safeguard on the future. Finally, although Ilyanovich had been hesitant to bring it up, Nakamura brought to Stinson's attention the fact that each of the current Directive member nations had been enemies of the United States in the country's relatively short history. Although very careful not to say so outright, Nakamura implied that the United States would be foolish not to join the Directive when it had the chance. Otherwise, the United States could never be sure what this organization, in which so many former enemies worked in collusion, would take it into its head to do next.

No fool, Stinson took Nakamura's meaning, and her argument had more impact on his reasoning than any other presented to him that afternoon. He took his copy of the Sternych Missive to Congress and the President, winning just enough votes to bring the United States into the organization. After only a short wait, Congress approved Stinson's proposed budget through the Department of Defense. Stinson called on the brightest agents of the Central Intelligence Agency and the National Security Agency and added their abilities and expertise to the Directive's efforts. He then nominated Arnold Harris, the Deputy Director of the Central Intelligence Agency (CIA), to act as his proxy in the day-to-day affairs of the Directive.

The Directive on the World Stage

Perhaps thanks to a lackluster introduction to the world at large, the Directive made barely a ripple on the surface of the public consciousness. Growing used to multinational cooperative efforts with little discernible function, naysayers and detractors of the Directive were relatively few. It was said, in fact, that the harshest treatment the Directive received in the public eye lay in its farcical portrayal in the Edward Blush movie, *No Go*, in which the organization seemed less competent than the Keystone Cops. By staying out of the spotlight and making few public appearances, the Directive failed to engender any of the broad-based suspicion that it's predecessors (the KGB, MI6, the CIA, the NSA, etc.) had been heir to. No one really seemed to know or care what the Directive was about. Conspiracy theorists from around the world turned their sights away from Project Utopia very briefly, only to discover that the Directive seemed just as concerned as they were. As far as many observers could tell, the Directive just didn't *do* enough to be a source of concern.

However, the Directive was very active during that time. The captains of the organization devoted the first two years of the program's existence to pooling information, laying out the standard operating procedures and hammering out the means by which the tenets of the Sternych Missive would apply to those procedures. Petr Ilyanovich had gathered a great deal of information on novas during the turbulent early years of Andrei Srebrianski's Presidency, even going so far as to organize a "collection" of Drs. Mazarin and Rashoud's notes on the phenomenon of nova "eruption." Although the co-opted information led Russian scientists to many of the same conclusions that Mazarin and Rashoud came to, Ilyanovich ordered the scientists to sit on the information until after Mazarin and Rashoud released their own findings. In that fashion, he reasoned, his scientists would have more time to examine the data, so as to give him more complete picture with which to work.

At the same time, Ilyanovich worked to uncover many of the measures the other G7 nations had set in motion at the outset of the Nova Age. His agents gathered intelligence on "nova-comparable" technology developed by the industrial giants, preliminary tests of nova military applications and the activities of unaligned novas in various theaters around the world. In the first two years of collaboration, Ilyanovich released much of this information to his partner nations, in order to show them just how widespread an effect novas were having on the world. The representatives of the other nations of the Directive used Ilyanovich's information as a foundation from which to build their own common storehouse of facts, projections and intelligence on the new world that had only begun to emerge.

Aside from information management, the Directive also engaged in an intense recruitment drive, drawing in agents from international intelligence organizations, federal police bureaus and the military. The size of the Directive ballooned to more than 70 active field operatives and a support staff salted throughout many law-enforcement and national security agencies in each of the member nations. The organization recruited its first nova agent, Lucas Barrows of the United States, in early 2004.

While it remained mostly covert and analytical in its early years, the Directive did fade in and out of the public eye regularly. Presenting itself as a check against aggressive nova terrorism, the Directive was often the first organization to

supply agents to trouble spots of national or international significance. Once every few months, the average citizen could find pictures in the news of Directive operatives in blue-and-white uniforms securing an area or mopping up after defusing a tense international incident. As time went by, Directive Blue and Whites even began to appear regularly in opposition to the rare Teragen protests and demonstrations that turned violent, casting itself as a protector of mankind second only to Project Utopia. The Directive employed the uniformed operatives only in high-visibility situations, in order to build a specific public image of itself as a highly organized, multinational force of global peacekeepers. The Directive did more work behind the scenes, upholding its true goal as a force of watchers, but the image it put forward maintained a more favorable public opinion.

However, the "Newsman Incident" of late 2004 brought the Directive to the notice of the entire world. The organization came to the particular attention of Chancellor Erich Galt, former German intelligence officer and former president of the *Universität der Bundeswehr* (Federal Armed Forces University) in Munich, who would be responsible for the inclusion of Germany into the Directive as its fifth member nation.

The Newsman

In July of 2004, Lucas Barrows, an American nova special agent in the Directive's employ, was assigned to monitor German communications and media output for evidence refuting or confirming rumors that German President Fredericksen harbored a personal prejudice and animosity toward novakind. Preliminary intelligence suggested that Fredericksen was one step shy of activating the German alert forces in an attempt to chase all active novas from Germany. No intelligence suggested why the President seemed to feel this way, but if the speculation was true, Fredericksen's actions would set a dangerous anti-nova precedent in Europe. If tensions between the German government and the European nova community got out of hand, the consequences could be disastrous.

However, none of the great volume of public-media information collected by Agent Barrows supported the closed-door rumors indicated by the Directive's covert collection. In fact, a great deal of press and media coverage of German novas spoke in glowing praise of the new beings. Pictures of Ilsa Dreiden — the first native German to erupt on German soil — practically littered the streets, and television specials on the services novas had provided to the German government appeared at least once a week. The German people, it seemed, were as in love with novas as the rest of the world.

The German Parliament had even taken steps to ensure the complicity of novas on German soil with German governmental initiatives. The Parliament had passed a law in 2003

imposing a tax on novas visiting Germany from other countries, with the proviso that novas who volunteered for temporary stints of community service were exempt from paying the tax. The revenue generated by the tax went toward paying Germany's baseline citizens to take on the initiatives that visiting novas chose not to. This law passed and, aside from isolated rallies by Teragen sympathizers, gained the acceptance of the German people easily. Those novas who simply decided to pay the tax, however, suffered lower popularity ratings in the German media, which convinced many of those to whom such ratings mattered to either stay clear of Germany altogether or reap the public-relations benefits of contributing to the German community when they did visit.

Still, despite the evidence suggesting that Germany embraced novas, Barrows was not convinced. On further investigation, he and his cell of operatives uncovered an odd connection underlying all the public attention given to German novas. That connection was Heinrich Keld, an independently wealthy German media magnate. Keld, it seemed, had paid for a great deal of airtime on national radio stations during which he commissioned speeches praising those novas who registered for government service. He wrote numerous editorials in the various newspapers he owned, urging novas to turn their incredible skills toward the betterment of Germany. His editorials and advertisements had generated much of the public approval for the new tax law. He even subsidized the production of many of the inspirational posters that became so familiar on German streets, showing familiar novas in matching uniforms (reminiscent of the German alert forces' uniforms) doing good around the community.

Famed for his incredible intuition, Special Agent Barrows approached Keld himself with worries that the wealthy publisher was forwarding a dangerous agenda. It seemed to Barrows that Keld had taken a stance in direct opposition to that which President Fredericksen had taken. Such a divisive move, Barrows explained, could polarize the German citizens' opinions, leading to potentially dangerous internecine conflict. For his part, Keld remained calm and collected, explaining to Agent Barrows how novas were the new hope for Germany — the beings who would propel the nation back to the status of world superpower, where it had been just 60 years ago. While many countries around the world shied away from actively recruiting their "aberrant" citizens into government service, Keld had launched his campaign to ensure that the people of Germany all but expected both their native novas and those who decided to settle in Germany to do their duty to the country. The *Bundesrepublik* would be strong again, Keld declared, and its strength would derive from its new *Übermenschen*. If Fredericksen could not see the wisdom in that ideal, Keld told Barrows, such a close-minded lack of vision was regrettable indeed.

Deeply disturbed, Barrows left Keld's office and reported to Director Harris and the other directors in charge. He let them know that his own active M-R node had detected high levels of quantum channeling from Keld and that even he had been almost swayed by the publisher's words. What was worse, the publisher's campaign had convinced a great many European novas of the merit in his initiative. Even Chancellor Galt himself had begun to express similar sentiments.

Fearing that just this sort of manipulation was afoot in his own country, Petr Ilyanovich approached President Srebrianski and told him the situation. Keld, a nova, was inspiring the creation of a German nova army rivaling any such force anywhere else in the world at the time. He begged Srebrianski to speak with President Fredericksen of Germany on behalf of a concerned Directive. After no great deal of convincing, Srebrianski arranged a private meeting with President Fredericksen. Having been more or less unofficially relieved of most of his public duties by Minister Sierka, Srebrianski flew into Germany and spoke alone with the German President. His arrival garnered little notice or fanfare.

Despite its monumental importance, the exact details of the meeting remain a closely guarded secret. The little information that Petr Ilyanovich has released to the Directive's other leaders states that Srebrianski presented to Fredericksen the evidence collected by Agent Barrows, as well as a summary of that agent's fears about Keld's motives. After being removed from direct exposure to Keld's influence, President Fredericksen became upset at what Srebrianski told him and ordered an immediate investigation by the alert forces of the German police and the Federal Criminal Police Office (the BKA). In order to demonstrate his good will, Srebrianski offered the aid of his Directive operatives under the command of Petr Ilyanovich.

Special Agent Lucas Barrows even offered to play a dangerous game of "chicken" with Keld's influence. Exposing himself to as much of Keld's subtly manipulative message as he could stand, Barrows decided to approach Keld a second time, claiming to have embraced the publisher's philosophies. Fellow nova operative Jesse Hooks coached Barrows in the art of clandestine infiltration and the means of keeping one's mind functionally divided so as to complete the mental disguise of an undercover identity (even if said identity was already one's own).

With teams of collection specialists in place beyond the walls of Keld's offices with laser microphones at the ready and German alert forces prepared to descend if necessary, Barrows went to speak with the man. Barrows told Keld that he had been spying on him for quite some time and that he had finally converted. Keld was not particularly surprised by this revelation, but he was shocked when Barrows told him that he had altered evidence and lied to his superiors on Keld's behalf. Barrows persuaded the publisher that the German hierarchy had been convinced that Keld was conspiring with the European nova community to overthrow the German government, starting with President Fredericksen. Barrows convinced the German that he had protected him thus far from the appearance of impropriety.

Keld prolonged his interview with Barrows for more than half the day, using every quantum-fueled resource at his disposal to try to catch the agent in a lie, but he found Barrows beyond reproach. However, the publisher informed Barrows that despite the agent's dedication to "the cause," he was not qualified to join in the glorious initiative that began with the betterment of Germany. Thus far, his plans involved only European novas, particularly Germans, and the Texan Barrows most certainly did not fit that bill.

Wary of giving the game away by seeming too eager to leave or not dejected enough for being turned down, Barrows almost left Keld's office. Before he could depart, however, Keld made him an offer. Although Barrows could not aid Keld in the *Neue Reich*, perhaps he could begin to spread the ideal to his superiors in his own country. Working in collusion with novas around the world toward one glorious vision (i.e., Keld's vision) would be a worthy endeavor indeed — certainly more so than the plastic façade put forth by Project Utopia. Where Adolf Hitler's insanity and bigotry had driven his goals of worldwide unification to ruin, Keld's goals would not fail.

Walking a dangerous line against Keld's every manipulative facility, Barrows drew out the particulars of the megalomaniacal nova's vision and his far-reaching plans to see that vision come true. Those plans involved removing President Fredericksen from office for his subtle paranoia and prejudice against novas. They called for the replacement of Chancellor Erich Galt, since the Chancellor had proven resistant to Keld's plans to allow many German government services to be restructured and/or replaced by the abilities of German novas. The plans even called for the creation of a nova-only force that's primary function would be to recruit novas from beyond Europe. Keld explained these goals to Special Agent Barrows and detailed his part in them, welcoming Barrows to what would be the *true* Nova Age of Germany — all while a veritable army of German alert forces and Directive operatives listened in mute shock.

Unable to maintain the charade any longer, Special Agent Barrows uttered the agreed upon code phrase. "Herr Keld," he said, "may this day remember the glory of the German republic." Moments later, a swarming mass of uniformed Directive agents and German officers of the BKA filled Keld's office. The operatives arrested Keld before the surprised publisher had a chance to speak.

After only the most casual pretense of a trial, Keld was found guilty of treason and conspiracy charges. He was then

sentenced to imprisonment at the Directive's Forgotten City prison facility. Many of the European novas who had volunteered for German civic duty under Keld's influence renounced their intentions when it became clear that they had been manipulated. Thus far, none of them has been indicted on conspiracy charges with Keld, though many are still under investigation.

Ironically, the German people did not approve of the actions of the Directive and the BKA. Keld's nationalistic supporters protested every day of the widely publicized trial, and several small-scale riots broke out on the day he was sentenced. In fact, the entire trial had to be set back when the judge presiding over the case declared it legal under the Basic Law to dismiss the sitting jury after Keld's impassioned testimony and sequester a new one to whom the powerful speech would be read by the court recorder. The four Directive member nations adopted the landmark legal precedent immediately thereafter.

The most ironic turn to the incident, however, was the fact that Keld's own media outlets made millions covering the story. It featured the actions of the Directive prominently, first in a negative Orwellian light. Yet, as Keld's outright influence began to fade and a measure of objectivity returned, the media portrayed the Directive in a more positive and heroic light. Keld himself did not suffer at the hands of his own loyal reporters and broadcasters, but the whole truth of his goals and agendas came out. In the space of weeks, nearly everyone on Earth had been exposed to the story and its chilling implications. Quantum power, the story showed the world, could be just as subtle as it was sensational. In the hands of a public servant, it could be well used and extraordinarily effective; in the hands of a misguided egoist, it could be devastating. Keld's delusions of grandeur had actually threatened to turn his idealistic agenda into a totalitarian regime enforced by the novas Keld had won over to his service. The publisher's actions had demonstrated that novas had a duty to use their abilities responsibly in service to the world. While such a responsibility should never be a forced requirement, as Keld's quantum manipulation had made it, responsible civic duty was certainly a noble end to which to direct one's exceptional capabilities.

Under different circumstances, the message was one of which even the subtle master manipulator Keld would have approved.

THE FORGOTTEN CITY

At the beginning of the 21st century, the city of Omsk in Russian Siberia had all but died. The Moscow Crash wiped out the viability of the city's factories and mining facilities, leaving more than 80 percent of the city's inhabitants desperate and homeless. Riots broke out, and only the intervention of the Russian military was able to quell the chaos.

As part of his economic plan that saved the Russian Confederation from outright dissolution, Vladimir Sierka took special notice of the city of Omsk. He melded what resources remained viable from Omsk's transportation, manufacturing and mining industry with those of nearby Novosibirsk, all within the boundaries of Novosibirsk itself. The combination of the two old-world hubs of Siberian industry proved feasible, thus helping to bolster the rest of Russia's flagging economy. However, while the admixture resulted in an enlargement of Novosibirsk and a general improvement of living conditions therein, it left Omsk all but empty. What few hangers-on in Omsk could not be integrated in the new industrial giant growing in Novosibirsk were relocated to more affluent parts of Russia closer to Moscow, where a shortage of workers made them necessary. Railroad workers diverted the Trans-Siberian Railroad away from Omsk, and the city remained there, abandoned.

Seizing what he saw as an opportunity, Petr Ilyanovich arranged for President Srebrianski in 2003 to co-opt that abandoned property for use by the Directive. It had occurred to him that, although the Directive had adopted measures for detaining dangerous novas who threatened the national interests of the its members, the organization had nowhere to put those it detained. The idea of putting a being of godlike power in a conventional jail cell was unacceptable, after all. The isolated and forgotten city of Omsk boasted numerous mines and industrial sites that could be converted into adequate holding facilities for far less than the cost of building the same from scratch. Within the year, construction and remodeling had begun.

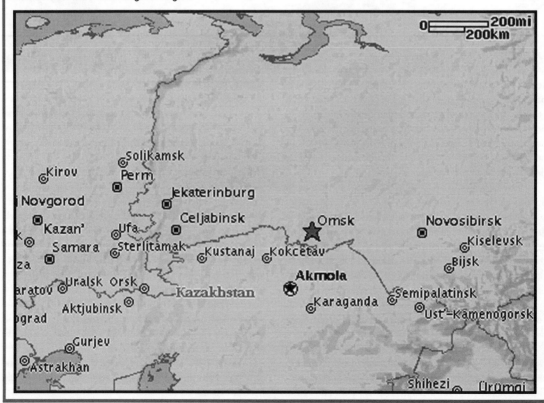

THE FORGOTTEN CITY, CONT.

Today, the Forgotten City serves two purposes. The residential areas of the city serve as housing and training grounds for probationary Directive operatives. They perform drills and practice maneuvers in the largely abandoned cityscape, simulating a wide range of scenarios that might arise in the urban landscape in which they will operate on a regular basis. The mines and industrial centers of the city, however, remain a prison for nova criminals with whom the Directive has crossed paths. Both hired nova elites and Directive novas of Omega Division act as guards at the facility as do numerous baseline military personnel armed with the latest in Japanese technology. Automated sensors, Klot tanks (see page 57) and electronic countermeasures have been installed at the facility to circumvent the threat of escape, and the nova prisoners there are dosed with quantum-suppressing moxinoquantamine regularly. Many are kept sedated as well.

A last-resort contingency has been installed at the facility as well, in case a truly desperate situation arises. The five directors of the Directive (Ilyanovich, Lathrop, Nakamura, Stinson and Galt) have access codes to an array of atomic devices that lies beneath the converted mines and industrial sites that now house those criminals who have been sentenced to imprisonment there. Should those explosives detonate, the destruction would bury the city, hopefully destroying whatever prisoners had caused such a desperate action to be taken in the first place. None among the Directive has yet laid out exactly what situation would necessitate the destruction of the Omsk facility.

The population of the city varies as the Directive recruits a fluctuating number of new operatives every year. The population of the prison, however, remains small. It is even rumored by the Russian media that some of the facility's earliest inhabitants have been rehabilitated and discharged. No member of the Directive has yet given a description of what conditions must be met in order to be released from the Forgotten City. What's more, none of the rehabilitated novas who have supposedly been released have come forward into the spotlight since regaining their freedom.

What the coverage of the "Newsman Incident" truly showed the world, though, was just how effective the Directive could be in a potential crisis situation. Furthermore, it showed the power of a mundane, baseline organization to stand up in direct confrontation against a nova force and coming out victorious. It showed many "baseline purists" that although novas were certainly a force to be reckoned with, they were not beyond challenge. While novas were certainly the hottest of hot-button topics, they did not make the world go 'round. Retreating back to the Russian Confederation in the wake of the incident, President Srebrianski instructed Petr Ilyanovich to make that point exceedingly clear to President Fredericksen and Chancellor Galt of Germany.

Ilyanovich did so by extending President Fredericksen the opportunity for Germany to join the four founding nations in the Directive. The Directive's other three member nations supported the idea, if somewhat warily, but Fredericksen refused outright. The motion actually moved through the German Parliament with remarkable alacrity, but the President gunned it down before it could become official. Considering what the Newsman had ostensibly tried to accomplish, the President felt that joining a worldwide organization with power to engender broad, far-reaching effects was the last thing that Germany needed at that time. The idea of employing nova operatives in the Directive's more high-risk cases also turned him off to the idea. If one nova could all but create nationwide policy just by writing good newspaper editorials, the President reasoned, an elite cadre of them working together for the most powerful nations in the world could only spell disaster. That being the case, he would not hitch Germany to such a doomed venture. The Newsman Incident had so fueled President Fredericksen's lingering distrust and suspicion of novas that he was unwilling to participate in any initiative with which they were involved as integral components.

Chancellor Erich Galt, however, was not nearly so prejudiced. Testing the winds in the German Parliament, Galt approached Petr Ilyanovich independently and made the agent an offer. Using connections he had made during his time as president of Munich's Federal Armed Forces University and his silent partnership in the Daimler-Benz Corporation, Galt made sure that German resources aided the Directive's efforts despite President Fredericksen's objections. He managed to generate significant financial support, as well as recruit a handful of operatives from the BKA, keeping it all carefully hidden from President Fredericksen and the German government.

The secret has since slipped to the public via a transcript of an American Supreme Court case in which a Directive agent had been called on to testify, but no action has yet been taken by the German government against Galt. The reason for Fredericksen's hesitation to punish this seemingly grave breach of governmental trust has yet to be determined.

The Future of the Directive

Aside from carrying out its original operating parameters, it is difficult to say what the leaders of the Directive intend to do as time goes by. The largest goal of the organization is to simply monitor the growth and evolution of the world's societies as the Nova Age continues. It is also possible that the five member nations are considering to expand the scope of the organization yet again, looking to China as the next potential addition. Operatives have already begun to trickle into that country to study baseline-nova relations, governmental nova regulations and the overall political climate of China in this changing time.

The only certainty is that so long as novas exist and possess the power to change the world, the Directive will continue right along behind them. It will continues to watch and learn and record until the time comes for it to act. And when that time comes, the Directive will be prepared.

Structure

Briefing File: Directive Organization
To: Gerhardt Schroeder
From: Sir David Wallace
Re: Restructured Directive Organization
Classified: Most Secret (Eyes Only)

Dear Gerhardt,

Welcome to our little enterprise. You and your nation's participation in our program does my old English heart proud. It is nice to see two old friends working hand in hand against the threat that faces us all. Although some of what I'm about to write repeats information we went over in person, I thought you might like to have the whole picture outlined in one place. As noted, this is a Most Secret document, meant for your eyes alone. Although it contains no details of current operations, it is, of course, best not to let anyone know just how we organize ourselves for the herculean task at hand.

The Directive, like the intelligence organizations that preceded it in the last century, organizes itself using the classic cell structure. You are not the first person to wonder at our decision. Normally, of course, intelligence agencies only use the cell system for running operations in hostile territory. Why model our entire organization thusly? Because, in a world populated with novas, everywhere qualifies as hostile territory. Our mission and duty puts us at odds not only with nova groups like the Teragen and Project Utopia, but all novas. Certainly, some novas do work for us, and others present no threat, but every nova represents a *potential* threat. Every one of them.

So we use the classic cell organization because the enemy truly is everywhere. A single nova could unravel all our secrets if we did not use the insulating structure of isolated cells. Although I know you understand the basics of the system, allow me to explain how it works for the Directive.

The Directive: At the top sits the Directive itself, the secretive ruling council whose members represent our sponsor nations: the Russian Confederation, the United States, the United Kingdom, Japan and, most recently of course, Germany. Besides the well-known figureheads that we all see from time to time on OpNet, I don't know who sits on the Directive, nor would I admit it if I did. They alone hold all of our activities locked in their minds and files. A nova skilled in manipulation or telepathy who learned their identities could destroy our organization. Thus, their identities remain hidden, even from high ranking officials like you and me.

The Administration: Like any essentially bureaucratic organization, we rely upon an effective administration to keep our mission on track. The Administration is, in and of itself, divided into different cells of a sort. Discreet divisions have no knowledge of anything that transpires outside their own area of interest. For example, although Resources Division supplies the cells with whatever they need, it has no knowledge of where the cells operate or what agents work in each cell. Likewise, Transport Division, which delivers the resources, has no idea what it is delivering nor exactly who is receiving it. In this way, a mole within one division of the Directive could never uncover sensitive data about another division.

Research and Development: One of our more recent additions to the Directive, one that I'm sure your nation can contribute to greatly, is our research and development arm. The problem facing our agents in the field is how to deal with novas, beings of unparalleled power and abilities, some of which are not always readily apparent. We need, in effect, to level the playing field through reliable, untainted technology. Although we employ some low-level novas, many (including myself) hope to someday purge our ranks of all these aberrant, potentially dangerous beings. Technology will let us achieve that goal. Our research teams work in complete secrecy, reporting directly to the Directive council itself. They have already produced some impressive tools, and although I have no knowledge as to who they are or what they're currently working on, I look forward to seeing whatever they come up with in action.

Intelligence Cells: The majority of our agents work within the confines of either an intelligence or operational cell. Intelligence cells process raw information gathered from our myriad sources around the world. This can include a wide variety of tasks, from analyzing radio intercepts and mission reports to watching N! all day, every day just to make sure we have an accurate picture of popular attitudes toward novas. Each cell receives raw data from sources unknown to it and passes its analyses on to superiors whose identities are equally obscure. Thus, should a nova penetrate any cell, it cannot effectively follow the ill-gotten information either up or down the chain of command.

The average intelligence cell has between a dozen and 50 members. They usually operate out of secure secret locations in major metropolitan areas (since novas tend to congregate in cities). Most have express orders never to interact directly with any nova under any circumstances. The risk associated with the agents' capture or even just casual thought leakage in the vicinity of a telepathic nova is too great. Instead, intelligence cells watch from afar, using satellite imagery, hidden cameras and listening devices, wiretaps and cell phone intercepts and hacking into any and all nova-related computer systems. The goal of all this work is quite simple: The cell must keep track of every action of every nova in their territory, every moment of the day and night. Simple to say that, not so simple to execute.

Operational Cells: As you well know, my friend, watching from afar is not always enough. Sometimes — often, in fact — our operatives must deal directly with novas. This is the most dangerous task we can undertake but also the most vital. In order to assess and neutralize the nova threat, we must be able to confront it. Of course, confronting it does not always mean engaging it head on. Like the matador in the ring, we step to the side as the bull charges. We dance and deceive until it grows tired, until it makes a mistake. Then we strike it down. Our operational cells do not fight novas in the streets, the cells come at the novas from unexpected angles, attacking where their foe is weakest. Our first rule for all operatives is this: Never confront a nova on its own terms.

There is no set structure for operational cells. The Directive council creates them as necessary, and most large cells form smaller sub-cells in order to effectively and securely carry out their assigned missions. For example, a hypothetical cell tasked with monitoring and, when necessary, combating the Teragen might have dozens of sub-cells assigned to individual novas known to be part of that terrorist group. These sub-cells would have no knowledge of each other, reporting only to the head cell. The head cell, while technically operational, would not actually engage the enemy, since its members possess knowledge that could bring down the entire sub-cell structure.

Operational cells usually work in concert with one or more intelligence cells, although they have no direct contact with any intelligence analysts or providers. Instead the operational cells simply get the fruits of the intel cell's labors. As a result, it occasionally happens that operational and intel cells assigned to the same region or target end up duplicating each other's

STEVE Ellis '99

work without knowing it (i.e., both tapping a nova's phones or monitoring its personal computing activities). This doubling of work might seem wasteful, but it is the price we pay for security, and security is something we can never compromise.

The cell structure demands that its member cells have a great deal of individual initiative and the freedom to act as necessary. Thus, an Operational cell has great latitude in carrying out its assigned tasks. In the face of the nova threat, a threat from beings that know no laws or international boundaries, the niceties of legal restrictions and constitutional constructs stand in our way rather than help us. Members of operational cells work secure in the knowledge that the only higher power they will ever answer to is the Directive itself. We provide all the protection they might ever need when it comes to possible "legal" ramifications.

Recruitment

Our dedication to security begins at recruitment. Although we naturally hope to bring German agents into our ranks as quickly as possible, we must do so in a cautious manner. You and several of your countrymen have mentioned repeatedly your desire to have full participation in the Directive's operations. I assure you, this will come in time, after the candidates you've proposed go through our entire vetting process. For your benefit, allow me to briefly outline the background check and recruitment process.

Monitoring

First of all, no one volunteers to join the Directive. We choose prospective members, almost always without them being aware of it. Working with us requires that an individual shares the same beliefs and goals as we do. While anyone who learned a fraction of what we know about the true extent of the nova threat would be horrified, we prefer to employ operatives who have already come to this conclusion on their own. We want committed men and women who are willing to take risks and do what needs to be done to secure our future — humanity's future that is, not the future of *Homo sapiens novus*.

As with all aspects of Directive structure, we have certain cells devoted solely to recruitment. They monitor intelligence agencies, military forces, police, private security firms, scientists and even journalists and academics around the world, looking for promising candidates. They pass on their recommendations to other cells, cells the recruiters have no other contact with. Our talent scouts never know whether or not any of the people they recommend actually become members of the Directive.

This second tier of cells evaluates the prospects and secretly monitors them for upward of six months, while running a full background check. Thus, possible recruits have already had their every move watched for weeks or months

and their security status thoroughly examined before anyone ever approaches them about working for the Directive. This process all but ensures that no moles or double agents work their way into our organization.

Vetting and Acquisition

Once a likely prospect has passed our initial checks, an operative approaches him about joining the Directive. Our operative usually poses as someone working for the potential recruit's government (or some other organization we know the potential recruit admires and respects). If the potential recruit agrees, he undergoes a series of mental and physical tests as well as a battery of interviews and more background checks. Applicants tend to be on their best behavior during this time, suspecting (rightly) that they are under 24-hour surveillance. Thus the importance of our initial, secret monitoring.

The potential recruit then undergoes a period of false recruitment, training and operational use. This is, in fact, another form of test, although the potential recruit has no reason to believe it is such. He thinks he's passed all the tests and is actually working for whatever agency he believes recruited him (at this point no one has mentioned the Directive). The training we give is useful and relevant, but in a more general sense: basic tradecraft or intelligence-analysis skills (depending on what he's being recruited for). During this period, our recruitment cells present their potential recruits with a number of "hidden" tests, occasions where the potential recruits are tempted to betray their oaths in some way. These range from blatant attempts to bribe the potential recruits to having "good friends" request a small piece of seemingly harmless, but nonetheless classified, information. Should the candidates fail any test we dump them from the program.

Only after several months of such testing does the recruitment cell actually admit any recruits into the Directive. At that point, the cell passes the recruits off to a training cell and never sees them again. Here again, our insulating cell structure keeps one hand from knowing what the other does, which, in our case, is a good thing. Recruiters have no idea what becomes of their recruits, what cells they end up working in or even if they pass through the entire training process.

The Nova Question

We prefer to recruit humans into the Directive's ranks. In fact, many think we should limit our recruitment to *H. sapiens sapiens* only. However, we do, on occasion, accept low-power novas. Novas in our employ cannot show any signs of taint or mental degradation. Furthermore, we never, under any circumstances, allow novas with dangerous and unstable quantum manifestations into our ranks. Our studies show conclusively that novas demonstrating "flashy" or "blatant"

powers, powers that twist the very laws of reality such as flight, energy projection, elemental manipulation and so forth are extremely unreliable and dangerous. The possession of powers at such a high level marks the nova as having mutated beyond humanity and, no matter what they might say or purport to believe, they are a threat.

The few novas in our ranks do not deviate significantly from our standards for humanity. They might well possess enhanced intelligence or social skills, and some even have mental abilities (which our studies say exist in humans without the M-R node). These low-level novas retain enough of their humanity to serve us, and their abilities can, sadly, prove crucial when facing high-powered nova threats. However, no nova can ever ascend very far within the Directive's ranks, and no cell can have a nova as its commander.

Training

You've been in this field for a long time Gerhardt, so I won't bore you with details on our basic training procedures. Suffice it to say, we give our operatives a firm grounding in intelligence gathering and tradecraft. Naturally, we have a variety of specialized training regimes with two areas of special interest: Electronic and Computer Intel is the first, Nova Relations is the second. I dare say that we excel in both far beyond any other military or intelligence agency in the world, except possibly Project Utopia in the latter field (but we're closing the gap quickly).

Electronic and Computer Intelligence

In the modern world, it is almost impossible to do anything without leaving some sort of electronic trace. Novas are no exception. In fact, because of their celebrity status and general wealth, they often leave more of a trace than humans do. All of our operatives receive extensive training in using the Directive's resources to track and analyze these electronic traces. Likewise, we learn how to make sure we don't leave a trace of our own for a nova or government organization to follow. Any one of us can read another person's e-mail or listen in on their phone conversations as easily as we can drive a car. Novas might have an advantage one-on-one in the physical world, but in cyberspace, our training and technology put us on the same level.

Nova Relations Training

Dealing with novas is always a dangerous, unpredictable undertaking. Even the best documented, most heavily profiled novas can, at times, be dangerously unpredictable. All Directive agents receive extensive training on how to deal with novas when and if they actually come in contact with one of these beings. The greatest danger from novas comes not from their ability to shrug off bullets or hurl death from their fingertips, in this they are no different from men in body armor wielding guns. The real danger comes from their powers to manipulate, their ability to read thoughts, the cloud they can throw over a person's mind. As members of an intelligence organization that lives or dies by the secrets it keeps, such abilities could be our undoing.

We teach everyone who passes through our programs some basic techniques to fight mental meddling. Self-hypnosis is the most valuable, a technique whereby our operatives can focus their entire consciousness on single thought, phrase or image, blocking out everything else from their minds so that a telepathic nova cannot gather any useful data. This technique works to varying degrees depending on the operatives' strength of will and commitment to the training. Some operatives can scarcely use self-hypnosis at all, while others can form nearly impenetrable shields in their minds.

The Directive also employs a series of hypnotic locks and keys within the minds of operatives with extremely sensitive information (such as cell leaders and other high ranking members). These locks are post-hypnotic suggestions that prevent the operatives from recalling certain facts unless the proper "key" triggers them. The key can be a word spoken by a particular person or seeing a certain place or even just being awake at a certain time and date. However, the most common use of these locks and keys prevents operatives from recalling information unless they're in a specific location, such as their local headquarters. This prevents casual scanning on the street or even questioning under duress from revealing secrets of the workplace.

Our R & D staff has also developed some interesting solutions, particularly when it comes to dealing with charismatic and seductive novas. It should be acknowledged that none of these methods are anywhere near foolproof and that a powerful nova can break down all the barriers we set up. Likewise, it is a well-established fact that, given enough time and the willingness to take the necessary steps, a questioner can always break a prisoner down. Eventually, all of us talk. Thus the cell system that insulates us somewhat from any damage resulting from a security breach. Fortunately, the same holds true for novas as well. None of them are immortal or unstoppable. All of them have their weak points. We have shown repeatedly that we can break them, and each time we do, we learn something new.

I hope this answers some of your questions Gerhardt. Welcome aboard and I look forward to working with you and your fellow Germans. You're a great asset to us all. Hopefully, the Chinese will see things in the same light soon as well.

Yours,
DW

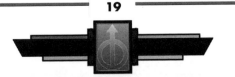

—from information packet 1A, distributed to potential Directive operatives

Congratulations on Being Invited to Join the Directive

Years spent collecting and analyzing data on the phenomenon of this new millennium bespeak the existence of certain undeniable facts. This world will not long remain that into which we were born. The pace of change outstrips even our most optimistic predictions. Beings of infinite potential and undeniable power walk among us and stride above us, advancing our species by decades every moment like shining Prometheus. There is much to appreciate in this period of history, but there is also much to cause us concern.

The information within these pages speaks to that concern. Too often, mankind is a slave to its own terrified imagination, and the potential for the entire species of *Homo sapiens sapiens* to succumb to such fear is great. Avatars of the primal cosmic forces of the universe walk among us, and they represent a decided threat to our continued stability. However, we do not fear. The novas of our world are fundamentally human, just as we are, and any threat that a human being can pose to the rest of his species is one that can be opposed by the rest of his species. This organization exists to safeguard mankind against any such threat and ease the transition to the time in which *Homo sapiens sapiens* and *Homo sapiens novus* need not fear one another.

The preceding files and dossiers have explained why you have been contacted in particular, as well as the ways in which your skills and talents are likely to benefit our endeavor. Consider your response to this invitation very carefully. We select our recruits with the utmost consideration, and we choose only those who show the potential to contribute to the goals and motivations of the Directive. You are under no obligation to accept our offer, but bear in mind that refusal could result in the loss of certain security clearances and reassignment to a different theater of operation within your current agency.

Please read this packet of information in its entirety before making a decision; you may ask any questions you may have of your recruiting agent after you have finished.

Goals of the Directive

As set forth in the Sternych Missive (1 May 2001), the goals of the Directive organization are as follows:

To Gather Information on Novas

These new beings are of paramount importance in the 21st century, and gathering information on them is the primary purpose of the Directive. The Directive exists to forearm the nations and people of the world against possible nova insurgency and terrorism, and the manner in which to best realize that ideal is to gather and analyze all pertinent data on them. We are particularly interested in the following questions:

How do novas impact the world?

As demonstrated by Vladimir Sierka's economic solution to the Moscow Crash, individual novas have the power to change the world. However, nova potential does not pertain solely to the political arena. Consider the novox singer Alejandra. With very little help, she created an entirely new genre of music within the entertainment industry. On a broader scale, look at the N! network. The mere existence of novas catalyzed a change in the worldwide cable-television industry, which has made many Indian and American entertainment engineers extraordinarily wealthy. The ways in which novas generate worldwide change are as varied as novas themselves, and we must prepare ourselves for every possible contingency.

The changes wrought by the presence of novas are often not so important themselves as the patterns of human behavior that iterate into the global consciousness in their wake. Our study focuses on the ways in which novas affect our world. Had Adolph Hitler or Pol Pot garnered more public support during their lives, we could be living in a very different world.

All novas have the capacity to be that effective and that persuasive, recruit, and it is up to us to monitor the means by which those beings exercise that capacity.

How are novas, themselves, changing?

We answer this question in two ways. The first deals with how the world in which the nova matures affects him psychologically. The second deals with the actual mutations the body and psyche undergo upon nova eruption.

The first is the most research-intensive, collection-oriented category of investigation one can undertake in the Directive's employ. There are approximately 9000 novas in existence (1 January 2010), and we compile and maintain computerized dossiers on as many of them as possible. Baseline psychologists and nova analysts funded on contract by the Directive itself update these dossiers with projections on future behavior, estimated levels of power and estimations on the subjects' potential to become national or worldwide threats. Operatives participating in this ongoing project are expected to know the novas to whom they are assigned as well as, if not better than, they know themselves. Operatives are expected to initiate intelligence-collection procedures including, but not limited to, the collection of MASTINT, COMINT, RINT and HUMINT pertinent to the subjects of study. An operative oversees every stage of the intelligence cycle and reports his findings and projections on his packet of novas to his department head every month. Through analysis of these raw data, Directive C3I in Moscow is able to compile psychological profiles of the world's novas, inasmuch as such a broad undertaking is feasible. This vigilance aids in the formation of immediate-action contingencies should the novas under surveillance make such measures necessary. Understanding how novas react to the world around them is essential to the Directive's core philosophy, a philosophy that can be summed up with the phrase, "Know thine enemy."

Understanding the physiological changes the human body undergoes during the process of eruption is a somewhat more quixotic goal, but it is no less important. In order to develop potential countermeasures against novas who would use their powers for illicit purposes, The Directive aims to catalogue the full range of nova capabilities. This undertaking includes viewing volunteer demonstrations by our erupted personnel; collecting IMINT, LASINT, PHOTINT and QRINT of novas in action; and monitoring the progress of nova-related research funded by the governments of the Directive's member nations. Covert collection of the latter form of data led to the discovery of the M-R node by Ivan Yaslov almost concurrently with Drs. Henri Mazarin and Farah Rashoud. For estimative intelligence on publicly demonstrated quantum capabilities, see the Appendix entitled "Capability and Potential of Quantum Manipulation" in Information Packet 2A.

A sub-section of the study of quantum "power" and nova psychology is the paraphysician specialty field of quantum abuse. The deleterious physical and psychological effects of channeling and manipulating quantum energy are rarely understood phenomena as of yet. However, Directive and civilian-sector scientists have begun an intensive study of them. The results of that study have not been compiled for publication as of the printing of this information packet.

///

Confused yet? Better hope not; you're going to be tested on this when your recruiter comes back. Didn't tell you that, did he/she? And all those acronyms are a pain in the ass if you don't have an intelligence background, but I marked the glossary with another note when I took the test, just like the guy before me did when he passed his manual on to me. That should help, but you'd better start reading more carefully. Read between the lines. Think about what phrases such as "Covert collection of the latter form of data" _really_ mean. Be sharp, recruit, or you're not going to make it. Oh, and get rid of these strips after you read them. Eat 'em, stick 'em in your shoe, whatever. Just don't get caught with them when your recruiter comes back.
—B

///

What are they doing?

Corrollary to the collection of estimative intelligence on how novas affect the world is the collection of current intelligence on the mundane activities of certain target novas. Much of this information overlaps with profile information collected for estimative purposes, but the ends to which it is used differ. Consider this information "reactive," whereas the preceding estimative data is "proactive."

Target novas of particular interest to the Directive include military elites, independent mercenary elites, members of Team Tomorrow, known members of the Teragen and all unaffiliated novas of threat-level Gamma or higher.

On a more general scale, this intelligence provides us a basis for understanding behavior patterns that have emerged in the Nova Age. We use this information to delineate nova-nova interaction as well as nova-baseline interaction. For instance, HUMINT and QRINT data shows that novas engage in a behavior labeled the "Ping Reflex" when coming into contact with each other for the first time. By emitting a pulse of quantum energy, novas are able to detect one another in much the same fashion naval vessels sending simplistic acknowledgements via active sonar do. By the same token, certain types of novas engender subconscious worship or panic responses in many baseline observers, and many novas of that type are quite adept at capitalizing on that reaction. The greater one's quantum capacity, it seems, the better able one is to create the desired impression in a baseline audience. However, it has been noted by multiple sources that novas are aware of this reaction on a conscious level, and they are quite capable of "playing against type" to allay those fears if they so choose. Heinrich Keld (AKA the Newsman) demonstrated this talent to undeniable effect, making himself out to be a civic-minded German nationalist, when he was, in fact, using his gifts to manipulate his audiences in order to further his own ambitions. Were it not for the efforts of certain American and RusCon Directive operatives, the situation might have degenerated into a much more serious international conflict.

Yeah, you're welcome.

Uphold Member Countries' Interests as They Relate to Novas

The Directive is an organization created by a coalition of independent governments outside the authority of Project Utopia and the United Nations. Similar to the North Atlantic Treaty Organization, the Directive strives to uphold the interests and national security of the member nations against a common foe. However, in the Directive's case, the common foe is less a direct threat than a *potential* threat. The Directive acts as a safeguard against both nova terrorism and Utopian aggression. Yet, far from antagonizing Project Utopia or opposing its goals outright, the Directive stakes out the political and economic boundaries of its member nations, outlining areas in which those nations will brook no Utopian interference.

At the same time, the Directive sees to its member nations' interests in other ways. Initiatives of this nature include the creation of an independent Interpol intelligence archive, aiding in the prosecution of international law and assigning operatives in advisory and supplementary capacities in matters of national security and international entente. Any threat to the safety and stability of our member nations is more than fair game. Furthermore, the government of each member nation supports the aims and goals of the Directive with cooperation and financial backing. Agents of the Directive are authorized to act in any member country on behalf of the Directive, so long as such actions do not conflict with the stated aims of the member country in which they act.

Safety Tips

This is stuff you don't get from reading between the lines, so pay attention. Here's how you act in the Dir's member countries to get what you want without getting static from the locals. This'll save you the trial and error most of us go through:

The "cause of freedom" is really all you need to remember in the United States. In many ways, America still sees itself as the new kid on the block, and it takes no shit. If you're acting in the States, make sure the authorities think you're helping get a bigger Big Brother (like Utopia) off their backs. If you step on toes and play yourself off as <u>the</u> authority in the situation, you're going to get stonewalled right out of any local assistance.

RusCon's a little different. Some Old Boys may feel betrayed or let down by Utopia, but it's not a hot-button topic for them. Where you're going to get bogged down is by saying you're operating on the President's authority. As far as most Russians are concerned, Sierka runs the show, and he's got the support in the Russian Parliament to push it if needs be. A lot of us don't trust Sierka, but most of the Russians do. And he can make things tough for you if you give him a hard time. Besides, he's a nova. Chances are, you're not going to be able to outsmart him on the fly. Stay out of his way, and keep your head down if you actually <u>are</u> acting on Srebrianski's authority.

The UK is a bitch. If you're going in, announce yourself well in advance, and make sure you've cleared your "visit" through both Vauxhall Cross and Thames House. The UK's internal Security Service (MI5) has a branch dedicated solely to making sure that Directive agents from other countries aren't poking around uninvited. In short, Britain wants to be left alone. In fact, the easiest time you'll have in the UK is convincing the gov't you're on a mission to extradite an international criminal. Otherwise, don't hold your breath waiting for British assistance.

Japan is easy. Be professional, be polite, and be discreet. And ask for help when you need it. The proper forms will get you assistance from Japanese police or even Nippontai, as long as you're specific in how such help will benefit Japan's national interest. Just remember, most of the nova "countermeasures" we use in the field come out of Japanese blacktech labs, the ones that are technically illegal under Utopian technology sanctions. Right now, we really can't risk alienating the Japanese.

And don't forget our bastard child, Germany. Do not approach German authorities unless it's a specific mission parameter. Keep your head in your shell on German soil. We do not have outright German government support. President Fredericksen turned us down, and Chancellor Galt went behind his back to hitch Germany to the Dir's wagon. We have the support of German industry and various sympathetic government contacts, but that's it, and it's all on the sly. The only help you're going to get from the actual authorities is if you can prove you're chasing Teragen activists out of Germany.

Protect Baselines

Although little publicized and seldom mentioned directly, the Directive exists primarily to protect those human beings who have not been so blessed as to erupt and become novas. We protect them not from some set antagonist but from the harmful changes being wrought by the turn of the new age. The entire world is changing, and its focus has shifted almost completely to the novas' spotlight. In such a climate, it is dangerously easy to let the concerns of baseline human beings wash away in the sensational tide of nova popularity. The Directive exists to see that such a thing does not happen. Novas are not inhuman, as members of the Teragen would have the world believe. All novas are human beings, and it is the purpose of the Directive to see that the laws of humanity apply equally to *all* humankind.

Other ways in which we protect baselines include:

Education

Fear is the greatest cause of concern in this age. Fear makes people rash and thoughtless. "Fear," as the American author Frank Herbert writes, "is the mind killer." And yet, fear is born most often from a lack of understanding. People who do not understand what novas are fear them as inscrutable beings of limitless capacity. Novas who no longer understand what it is like to be baselines fear them as jealous, spiteful monkeys. Those who do not understand the goals and methods of Project Utopia fear it as a totalitarian juggernaut. Those who do not understand the Directive fear us as the *Schutzstaffel* of the 21st century.

Therefore, the Directive engages in public-minded initiatives designed to help educate the masses on the state of the world as it changes around them. The organization encourages international cooperation in research on nova physiology and on the psychological impact of nova eruption. Much of our own intelligence and research data supplements these projects (covertly) as well.

Sure. Okay. Check out the Directive's budget allocation on that one if you get a chance. We leave the research up to our member nations' scientists. When they come up with useful field information, <u>then</u> it ends up in Directive hands. When we come up with something interesting in the field, we hand the data over to the researchers. They don't ask how we got it; we don't ask how they arrive at their conclusions about it.

Upholding Baseline Rights

In order to protect baselines from Utopian and rogue-nova aggression, there must be some standard against which to measure questionable actions. The original member nations of the Directive laid out this standard in the Sternych Missive, and each new member nation must agree to the terms set forth therein. Amendments to these rights can be approved only by a unanimous vote of the representative council of the Directive's member nations. Those rights assured to baselines include:

1.) The right to the necessities of life.
2.) The right to be judged according to a unified standard.
3.) The right to privacy.
4.) The right to safety.
5.) The right to be strong or weak without fear of reprisal.
6.) The right to reproduce.
7.) The right to independent thought.

These rights are the standards by which the Directive acts, and violations of them are grounds for prosecution by Directive authority and the laws of the governments from which it derives said authority.

Attorneys and legal theorists employed by the Directive have made great strides in setting legal precedents supporting this standard in courts around the world. Many of these rights have formed the basis for national laws in the United States and Japan, which had been untouched previously except by association. An application of the second listed right helped defeat a proposed American Constitutional amendment (27 July 2005) stating that recently erupted American citizens would have to be naturalized as Americans again, despite their status as citizens prior to their eruption. Although this product of then-President Pendleton's supporters in the house was sure to have been defeated, the proposed amendment held a great divisive potential that would have done nothing but sow hard feelings and xenophobia in the American nova community. Even discussing such a measure set a dangerous example for other, less democratic, countries around the world.

Actually, it's funny. The seven rights there could pretty much apply to the Teragen too. From what we learned in our early research, T'gen novas advocate personal freedom and their own rights, but their methods are completely different. Where as we work with the governments of the world to see that people are treated as they should be, Teragen novas draw a line in the sand and dare any nation in the world to step across.

Eliminating Threats

The least practiced, though perhaps most important, goal of the Directive is the elimination of threats against national and international security. The Directive concentrates its resources primarily on the objective of gathering information, but contingencies remain in place to deal with situations in which the national interests of the member nations are jeopardized or the basic rights of mankind are infringed upon.

The Directive applies force in eliminating threats based on a scale determined by the original four member nations. Other factors moderating the use of force include questionable jurisdiction, poor relations with the country presenting the obstacle and just bad timing.

Questions of jurisdiction occur when multiple member nations of the Directive claim a national interest in the matter at hand and the interests oppose one another. Jurisdictional issues also arise when no member nation can claim a direct interest in the situation, and no sufficient case can be made that human rights are being violated. By the same token, poorly kept extradition treaties or a history of poor relations between member nations and nations of interest to a Directive goal also hamper expedient use of force in unstable situations. For instance, Ibiza has proven reluctant to aid Directive personnel on numerous occasions, which increases dramatically the likelihood that Directive operatives found operating there covertly will be arrested or made the focus of an international incident. Although no nation has yet impeded the Directive outright, novas claiming asylum in a country with which no Directive nation has an extradition treaty are effectively beyond our reach. Finally, there is often no accounting for the timely arrival of the national military, retained elites or even Team Tomorrow in a well-supervised Directive operation. Very often, the time required to establish the Directive's presence and authority in a given situation exceeds the window of opportunity for the operation. If such is the case, the sacrifice of said presence and authority is worthwhile, so long as another capable agency solves the problem at hand.

And if you believe that....

Just make sure you never ask why we withheld our suspicions about Keld from the rest of the world before we moved on him. It's not the most famous case in Directive history for nothing.

Don't get me wrong, we'll call off the Blue and Whites if push comes to shove with another agency, but those operatives only make up the face we show the public.

Threat levels and priorities are as follows in the abridged chart:

Threat Level	Description	Recommendation
Alpha	No Threat	Standard Procedure
Beta	Potential Threat	Increase surveillance; increase COLEMP
Gamma	Subject of Concern	Round-the-clock surveillance; plan contingencies; assign reaction teams
Omega	Definite Threat (baseline)	Alert national security force; organize and employ appropriate reaction teams
Titan	Definite Threat (nova)	Alert national security force; alert Directive C3I; organize and employ appropriate reaction teams

Methods of eliminating threats take three basic forms of varying severity. The determination of when to apply each of these methods occurs during the Gamma stage of threat-assessment.

Social Management

The least confrontational methods of eliminating threats to Directive goals include those that affect a target socially. The idea of "social management" derives from the theory that linking a particular societal reaction to a set of behavior will generate a predictable response on the part of the perpetrator. The two methods of reacting to a threat in this way focus on positive and negative reinforcement, respectively. The desired result determines whether the subject is to be managed in a positive or negative manner. Social management can be most easily applied to threats of Beta and Gamma level. Higher level threats usually require more intensive measures.

The theory of using positive reinforcement to deal with an obstacle runs a dangerous ethical gauntlet, therefore Directive agents employ it less often. However, by playing to human greed and complacency, which applies to baselines and novas equally, a Directive operative can achieve certain goals both easily and expediently. Methods of positive social management include bribing informants, assigning sinecure government jobs to potentially disruptive individuals, arranging private funding for business or entertainment ventures initiated by the target or engaging in the more esoteric behavior known as "catering." Catering, in this sense, refers to the fulfillment of the more obscure desires of the subject to achieve a particular goal. Historically this has involved providing security for the loved ones of an information source who later testified against a rogue elite in British court, paying for the wedding of the daughter of an erstwhile aging political dictator (who then allowed Directive agents open access to his country's intelligence archives) and calling in a favor with a contact within Project Utopia to have that organization's Team Tomorrow branch grant an interview to a former DeVries Agency employee in return for that nova's assistance in tracking down a suspected Teragen terrorist.

Positive social management must be cleared with Directive C3I, and it must be presented to the potential subject forthrightly, so as not to give the appearance of corruption. Directive financial records involving positive social management are available upon request and open to inspection by United Nations' oversight committees, as well as to the legislative bodies of the Directive's member nations.

Negative social management, however, is almost universally covert. It is also dangerous, as it casts the Directive in a disreputable light to those who do not understand the necessity of such tactics. This practice includes such methods as blackmail, enforced ostracism, financial tampering and reputation engineering. Often, the Directive does not reveal its presence to the management subject until well after the negative management methods have been enacted. At that point, operatives may approach the subject offering what appear to be the tools of positive management in return for assistance or information. This two-tiered form of management works particularly well in India, where the film entertainment industry is a potent force in the country's economic structure. By putting subtle economic pressure on the Indian film industry (often through contacts in the American film industry), the Directive can cause temporary "dry spells" in that market, thus creating an indirect economic sanction on that country from the inside. By then offering covert funding to select powerful film producers through a screen layer of contacts or undercover operatives, the Directive pushes said producers to put economic pressure on uncooperative government contacts on the Directive's behalf. Less elaborate measures have proven equally effective.

Does "...the loss of certain security clearances and reassignment to a different theater of operation..." ring a bell?

Psychological Management

Psychological management is often more straightforward and effective than the more delicate social management. This method of threat-elimination is often supplementary to the social and overt physical forms of management, in that it attempts to force the subject in question to think and react a certain way to prearranged stimuli. Directive image specialists also apply this form of manipulation to the assignment of teams of uniformed Directive agents in order to make sure that the public image of the Directive in certain theaters is appropriate to the Directive's goals in those theaters.

Methods of individual psychological management vary in severity and focus. Information relating to certain targets' psychological states or mental triggers, gathered by collection operatives, is disseminated to management operatives who then use that information to engender predictable responses. For instance, a paranoid target can be manipulated to withdraw from his surroundings through an arranged information "leak" that reveals that he is under surveillance. This withdrawal and isolation can then make him easier to protect or abduct, as mission parameters dictate.

The classic use of psychological management applies to the interrogation of captured or otherwise hostile sources of information. A well-played interrogation should garner all

available information from an informant with a minimum of active resistance. Understanding the interrogation subject's psychological profile greatly improves the chances of directing an interrogation successfully.

A corollary use of this application of psychological management is that of resisting interrogation in the event of detainment while on assignment. Directive agents receive training in meditative resistance, and at the Directive's request, Kuro-Tek is developing a neurochemical inhibitor that will aid in resisting nova telepathic assaults.

The active use of psychological management techniques to uphold the public image of the Directive must be carried out with the utmost care and subtlety. The Directive is not a clandestine organization, although its operatives must often act with extreme discretion and subtlety. Therefore, in this age of instant satellite news broadcasts and OpNet information clearinghouses, we must maintain a noble, memorable public image. The image, however, needs not always match the reality, and it is in such instances where the two do not match that broad-scale psychological management techniques must be applied. Press conferences and filmed news appearances affect the public consciousness equally, as do OpNews press releases. Operatives often arrange such exposure through friendly contacts in the news media, although some agents can be called upon to create them independently. News of Directive operations in progress can be suppressed to prevent leaks of sensitive material. Certain efforts can even be delayed or extended so as to assure proper representation in the news. Heroic operatives are often assigned to "clean-up" missions after tense, well-resolved operations simply to get their faces on the news. Manipulating various aspects of our public image (being the first to arrive on the scene of a crisis, arriving in tandem with government troops, operating side by side with Team Tomorrow on occasion) is essential in building a rapport with government officials and in convincing potential aides that the Directive achieves its goals and is worthy of worldwide trust and cooperation.

Heh... just try "cooperating" with Team Tomorrow once, and see what their image is of your interference. Nobody appreciates a tag-along who's underfoot or a whiner who can't take care of his own messes. Remember that.

Overt Physical Management
Every tense international situation and every situation in which a person or group represents a threat to the achievement of the Directive's goals has the potential for an outbreak of some sort of violence. When diplomatic efforts fail to resolve such a situation, and both social and psychological management techniques prove fruitless, overt physical management is the only recourse. Overt management methods apply most often to situations of Omega- or Titan-level threats, and they are almost universally kept from public view. Gamma-level threats also warrant physical management if the window of opportunity in which to deal with the concern is finite and no other options remain. Arresting suspected malcontents and terrorists without sufficient evidence, in hopes that the arrest itself will turn up the missing proof, is an example of this application of force at the Gamma threat-level. Other uses of force at varying threat-levels include arresting known international criminals, altering the political structure of uncooperative non-member nations to create new infiltration opportunities, abducting reluctant information sources and eliminating Omega- and Titan-class threats. The operatives who carry out these management initiatives fall into three categories: blue-and-white hunter teams, covert operatives and contracted elites.
•Blue-and-White Hunter Teams
These teams make up the bulk of Directive agents with whom the public is familiar, primarily because they largely exist for show. These operatives wear distinctive uniforms, carry identical equipment and follow a precise code of conduct. They are responsible for maintaining the public image of the Directive at all times. Their actual duties include making arrests, securing areas of potential conflict, organizing and coordinating local police and military efforts and performing rescue operations in dangerous situations created by targets of Directive surveillance. The greatest proportion of Directive nova agents works alongside baseline operatives on these blue-and-white hunter teams. Blue and Whites are rarely put into situations where conflict is likely to escalate.

- Covert Operatives

The number of covert Directive operatives equals the ranks of hunter teams in the field. Covert ops work alone or in cells of specially assigned operatives whose applicable skills complement one another. Although it is not unheard of for novas to work as covert ops (as American Special Agent Lucas Barrows does), more than 90 percent of the Directive's covert ops are baselines. While many nova abilities prove useful in the field, nova subjects of observation can often detect hidden nova operatives via the aforementioned Ping Reflex. Thus, it is easier to insinuate baseline operatives "into the scenery" of a nova subject's life without arousing undue suspicion. Covert ops must, however, be especially careful in monitoring nova subjects, as such subjects are often well-equipped to detect mundane forms of intrusion that even seasoned baseline espionage professionals would normally miss.

Aside from the standard actions involved with the collection of intelligence, covert operatives also play a valuable role in physical management initiatives. These operators engage in abduction/replacement operations, assassinations, proactive anti-terrorist operations and the clandestine manipulation of the government resources of non-member nations in accordance with Directive goals. Most covert ops within the Directive work with official authorization and identification, thus easing them out of trouble with government officials if they are apprehended in the line of duty. These operatives can expect Directive assistance in such circumstances, as long as it can be proved that they were acting under direct orders. Certain operatives within Omega Division on missions of the utmost secrecy and sensitivity, however, forego that blanket of protection.

Which means they're pointed at their target and forgotten about. And they'd best accomplish their objectives with a minimum of fuss. Otherwise, they'd better have some good friends among the Blue and Whites, because that's who the Dir is going to send in to "clean up" the mess.

- Elites

In the event that no blue-and-white teams or covert ops are in position to handle an immediate threat (i.e., one of Omega or Titan class), the Directive maintains a small list of elites upon whom it can call. It is among the elites on this list that the Directive relaxes its restrictions on employing nova operatives who have been mutated by quantum abuse. The list includes "retired" Directive novas, reliable elites who are attached to the military forces of the Directive's member nations and individually contracted specialists.

Training of New Directive Operatives

In the attached files, you will find your service record and the rationale behind invite you to join the Directive. Doubtless, you have skills and abilities deemed either necessary or beneficial to the achievement of the Directive's stated goals, and your potential superiors in Directive C3I consider you a potentially valuable asset to the organization. However, despite the extensive training you may have already received in your current occupation, you will undergo further training for the first six months of your employment. This training will inform you of the specifics of the procedures outlined previously, as well as imparting upon you the minimum standard scope of skills and abilities that all Directive operatives must uphold. It is Directive policy to make sure that each agent is capable of taking on any other agent's role during standard operations. In this way, we demonstrate that no one individual is indispensable to our efforts and that the best way to gain the respect of your fellow operatives is to excel in your own performance through diligence, rather than by being chosen to reign over them.

God love 'im, Petr's trying to be clever here. Unfortunately, the fact of the matter is that the Directive just can't afford to employ specialists in every field it dabbles in. Nor can it always count on the specialists employed by the governments of its member nations. After all, they've got regular jobs, too.

Office Work

Although a large proportion of Directive operatives remain active in the field throughout most of their careers, the work done "in the office" is equally important to the intelligence effort. An understanding of the manner in which this work is done will give you insight into how your information is processed and how the information you receive in the field has been derived.

You will first be taught the methods and standard operating procedures the Directive employs in achieving its goals. More intensive than this overview, that information will present specific cases and specific details on when and how to utilize the resources at your command. Exact methods of the three forms of management will be discussed, as will the appropriate surveillance tactics to be used in situations of varying threat levels. Should you join an Alpha Division mission team, you will also be drilled in the proper codes of conduct and the schools of thought from which they derive. Finally, you will learn the proper paperwork that must be completed in various collection situations and the proper channels of communication that must be followed at all times.

The training also includes an overview of the methods of data analysis used by office workers in the Directive's employ. Making conclusions and decisions based on basic intelligence is extremely important, and every Directive operative must know how to do so in the field without having to rely solely on office information. This training also includes a study in creating psychological profiles, a skill that is invaluable in second-guessing a subject or making spontaneous field decisions.

The final portion of this training involves basic education in matters of utmost importance to any Directive agent. The first subject is that of nova physiology. The Directive was created in reaction to the onset of the Nova Age, and it only stands to reason that novas are a constant area of interest to Directive operatives. To better understand those with whom we so often concern ourselves, you will be provided with current information on nova physiology, the physics of quantum manipulation and its possible side effects. Simultaneously, you will be trained in modern computer science. Our instructors will drill you in every aspect of computer and information science from programming to directing OpNet searches to intrusion and security. The Directive employs many computer databases and conducts much of its international investigation via computers, and an agent without a basic understanding of that medium will not be able to function as a part of the organization. The final stage of the operative's education in the office includes a course on international law, including extradition, jurisdiction, existing treaties between nations, working with the United Nations and the rights and responsibilities of Project Utopia.

You can sleep through that first six months as long as you read your manuals, frankly. What you don't remember isn't going to kill you. Once you go into the field, you're going to be thrown in with veterans who've been doing this for years. Remember and take to heart your field training. Take extensive notes on the office info.

Field Work

The bulk of your training as a Directive operative will cover fieldwork, and it will be conducted in the field itself. You will be tutored in languages by native speakers and instructed in survival by individuals who live in the environments you will be operating in. Survival, in this context, refers to learning the culture, whereabouts of resources and specific taboos in various urban and rural environments. This training will enable you to better blend in with locals in your theater of operation as well as create more believable cover identities as the need arises.

You will also be taught the basics of investigation, surveillance and covert collection, if you have not been recruited from an organization that practices those techniques. This segment of your field training includes familiarization with the latest technological advancements in the field of surveillance, like the laser microphone, over-the-horizon radar and enhanced-capability countermeasures designed to foil a nova's heightened senses.

The last segment of your preparatory field training covers the areas of self-defense and weapon-use. Additional tests become necessary depending on which division you are assigned to as an operative, but you must maintain a minimum proficiency in basic martial arts and firearms operation throughout your career with the Directive.

Your Decision

You have performed your duties for your current employer admirably to date, and it is an honor to be chosen for recruitment into the Directive. A place exists for you here to further your skills and expand your duty to a global scale. We have not chosen you frivolously, nor have we chosen in haste. Your skills will be a valuable asset to upholding the principles on which the Directive is founded. Your place here is secure, regardless of your current level of aptitude. However, you are under no obligation to accept our offer. Think carefully on your decision until your recruitment liaison returns. Consider your duty; consider your sense of responsibility. We are proud to make you this offer to join us, and we eagerly anticipate your answer.

Hope you are/have been destroying these notes, recruit. Your liaison's probably on his way right now to administer your test, and it wouldn't look good to have all these scraps of paper lying around. In any case, this is the glossary marker I promised. Hopefully this info is stuff you already knew so you haven't been wasting your time flipping back and forth. Whatever. Good luck on the test.
     —B

GLOSSARY

ACOUSTINT	(Acoustical Intelligence) Information gained from the collection and analysis of sound
actionable intelligence	Information of immediate use after collection without needing analysis
ad hoc	A new requirement to address a recent or fleeting need during an operation
analysis	The examination of information for significant facts and probable conclusions
AOR	Area of Responsibility
asset	Any resource at the disposal of an organization for use in a support role
basic intelligence	General, factual reference material that concentrates on background and description
C3I	Command, Control, Communications and Intelligence
clandestine collection	The acquisition of information in ways that ensure the secrecy of the operation
COLEMP	(Collection Emphasis) The priority of a collection requirement
collateral	All available information not worked formally into the compartmented structure of the agency using said information
COLOP	Collection Opportunity
COMINT	(Communications Intelligence) Information derived from the analysis of communication intercepted by listeners other than the intended recipients
compartmentation	The system of restricting access to sensitive material and operations
counterintelligence	Information gathered to protect against espionage, sabotage, assassination and other similar activities
covert actions/operations	Clandestine activity designed to influence hostile or unwitting subjects to favor one's own motives and goals

CRITIC	An indicator that a message contains information of immediate importance
current intelligence	Descriptive information on dynamic, time-sensitive conditions and interpretation of the impact of said conditions
EEI	Essential Element of Information
ELINT	(Electronic Intelligence) Information derived from the study of electromagnetic radiations not dealing with communication, atomic detonation or quantum
estimative intelligence	Information that attempts to predict the future based on basic and current intelligence
exploitation	Obtaining information from any source and taking advantage of it for intelligence purposes
HUMINT	(Human Intelligence) Information derived from human sources
IMINT	(Imagery Intelligence) Information comprising products of imagery interpreted for intelligence use
intelligence	Evidence and conclusions acquired and furnished in response to known or perceived information needs
intelligence cycle	The process of collecting, processing, analyzing and disseminating information to suit a known or perceived need
Interpol	(International Police) Cooperative effort by international law-enforcement agencies to share information
IO	Information Objective
IPOLAR	(International Police Archive) The Directive initiative to compile a common storehouse of nova law-enforcement information accessible to all Interpol nations for use in expediting information exchange
LASINT	(Laser Intelligence) Information gleaned from laser surveillance devices
MASINT	(Measurement and Signature Intelligence) Intelligence incorporating acoustic, radioactive, infrared and electro-optic sensors to record and identify the unique characteristics of a particular platform
monitor	To observe, listen to, intercept, record or transcribe any form of communication or media for intelligence purposes
national security	The territorial integrity, sovereignty an international freedom of action of a particular nation
NIP	(Notice of Intelligence Potential) An indicator that a message contains news of a fleeting collection opportunity beyond the scope of the original collection assignment and that the operative is requesting instructions on whether to proceed
Office, the	A nickname for the section of the Directive that carries out data analysis, recruiting and the assignment of operatives
open-source information	Information of potential intelligence value that is available to the general public
OTHR	Over-the-Horizon Radar
overt collection	The acquisition of information from media, observation and the open sharing of data
PHOTINT	(Photographic Intelligence) Information gathered from photographs and evaluated for intelligence use
QRINT	Quantum Radiation Intelligence
RADINT	Radar Intelligence
Reconnaissance	Operation to obtain information on a particular area or s ubject by visual observation or other detection methods
REL	(Releasable to _____) An indicator of operatives to whom compartmented information can be released
RFI	Request for Intelligence
RINT	Radiation Intelligence

sanitization	The process of editing or altering information or reports to protect sensitive, privileged information within a widely distributed medium
SCI	(Sensitive Compartmented Information) Information requiring special controls for restricted handling
SIGINT	Signals Intelligence
SII	Statement of Intelligence Interests
social management	Method of exerting subtle social pressure on a subject in order to encourage cooperation with one's motives and goals
source	Any person, thing or activity that provides information
strategic intelligence	Information required for the formulation of policy or military plans
surveillance	Systematic observation or monitoring of places, persons or things by visual, aural, electronic, photographic or other means
tactical intelligence	Information required for the planning and conduct of tactical operations
target	An entity against which operations are conducted
undercover operation	Operation carried out using a false identity or other means to hide the intent of the operation or affiliation with the sponsoring organization.

The Test

All right, recruit, it seems that you've had plenty of time to read over the introductory packet. I am Special Agent Lucas Barrows, your recruitment liaison for the Directive. I get the impression from the excited look in your eyes that you've already made up your mind about whether or not to join us, so I won't ask. I am, however, going to ask you a few questions to determine your qualifications and exact placement within the organization. You look like you were expecting a test. That's good.

Ready? The test only has three questions, and you don't even have to write out the answers.

One: Who wrote the information packet you just read?

Two: How many strips of paper were in the packet when you started reading it?

Three: Judging from what you know about the Directive, who wrote the notes that had been left in the book for you?

Well, what're you gawking at, recruit? You've got five minutes to give me your answers. And I expect you to explain how you came to your conclusions.

<Transcript of a lecture by Professor Vance Daley given to five new recruits training in the United States>

We only exist because of our enemies. If there were no novas or, somehow, novas presented no threat, then there would be no need for us. But of course, there are novas, and some are most definitely threats. Thus, it is our enemies who in many ways continue to define us. We can only react to them and what they do. This is the age-old problem that has faced police and security organizations for millennia. Unless we are willing and able to lock up or neutralize the entire nova population, we must wait for them to make the first move. Our job is to anticipate that move, be ready for it and check it before it begins.

The real conundrum is that the Directive has no enemies. That is to say, not in the traditional sense. Even the fearsome Teragen does not qualify as an enemy organization, since it does not qualify as an organization at all. Some of us still remember the Cold War, a time that set the standards for intelligence gathering operations. Many of our leaders are in fact veterans of that war. In those days, no matter which side you were on, you knew who the enemy was. Then came the 90s, a decade that paved the way for the nova threat of today. It was the decade of terrorists and extremists: fundamentalists in the Middle East, nationalists in Eastern Europe, separatists in Northern Ireland and militia groups in the United States. The 90s taught us to root out the enemy within.

This last struggle was merely a prelude to the challenges we face today. Where once the threats separated into identifiable racial, cultural or political extremist groups, now they lurk among us under every conceivable guise. Some are celebrities, some infamous, some wear masks, others look just like you and me. Only a few look like the monsters they truly are. These novas are the enemies that define the Directive, and we are as multifaceted as they are. To those who seem law abiding, we are like the police: waiting and watching, ready to step in when they cross the line. To those known terrorists or those who conspire against humanity, we are a stalwart foe: engaging them in a fight for humanity where the stakes are so high, no cost is too great for victory. These then are our enemies, and this is who we are.

The Teragen

As I mentioned earlier, the Teragen scarcely qualifies as an organization (or so they would have us believe). According to Divis Mal's so-called *Null Manifesto*, it is a philosophical or intellectual movement, a group of like-minded thinkers. There is no acknowledged leader; its members have no admitted meetings or councils of war. They even claim to be nothing more than a Civil Rights Movement for novas, not unlike the American Civil Liberties Union in the United States. More-

over, since they do not admit to having a central authority, no one stands up to take the credit or blame when one of the Teragen's members does something decidedly evil. It seeks to be a movement without consequences, an organization without responsibility, which cannot thus be held accountable.

The Teragen's public stance does not fool us. We see it for what it is: a terrorist, nova supremacist group that sees humans as inferior beings. *The Null Manifesto* itself says as much, and the Teragen's members have gone on to show us just what they think that means. Admitted Teragen members around the world have carried out atrocious attacks of every sort on innocent humans. From rape and murder to destruction of property and mental manipulation, these terrorist monsters claim that humans are no more than animals compared to them. They say that a nova killing a human should carry no more penalty than one would accrue by killing a dog.

It is no wonder then that we have made combating the Teragen threat one of our primary missions. The Directive maintains what is surely the most comprehensive listing in the world of known and suspected Teragen members, and we watch each and every one of them as best we can, night and day. Naturally, we have much more success within the confines of our member nations. In the past year, Teragen outbreaks in the United States and the other Directive-affiliated countries have gone down, while elsewhere in the world, the average of Teragen sponsored or promoted incidents has risen in the same time period. Obviously, we are having an effect.

With such a success rate, no one was surprised when the Directive itself became a target for these terrorists. We not only expect such a response, we welcome it. Public statements from known and admitted Teragen members continue to decry our organization as "cryptofascist," "evil" and "dangerous." The last is certainly true, at least as far as the Teragen is concerned. The more resources Teragen members focus on fighting us, the less they have to attack the good people of the world. Their attacks against us have thus far failed to penetrate our networks or cause any serious harm. Moreover, in the course of its fight, the Teragen ends up sullying its own image even further, since its members often assault us in the open where the entire world can see their actions. When the attacks aren't public, we make sure that they become so.

It is a public relations war the Teragen cannot win. Despite the worldwide craze over novas as celebrities, humans still fear these super-powered beings. Our own information networks make sure that the popular press knows every instance where the Teragen commits some atrocity or another. Even when no known member takes credit for the act, our operatives ensure the media gets our version of the truth. Although certain gifted speakers amongst the novas have managed to convince many in the public that the Directive is

somehow sinister, we continue to give better than we get. Nova approval ratings in all four charter member nations are at an all time low, according to our polls.

Behind the Scenes

So much for the public battle. Unlike our enemies, we do not like to air our dirty laundry in public. As much as we might tip the media off about confirmed and suspected Teragen members, we play most of our cards close to our collective chest. The Teragen does not and must not know how much we really know about them and their organization. Our analyses indicate that we have identified close to 80 percent of the Teragen novas in our member nations and 55 percent of those in the world at large, many of whom do not publicly proclaim their allegiance. We watch and take action against them as necessary. These novas, by their very nature and their own proclamations, make the local justice systems inapplicable, and so, in this case, we abide by their wishes. If they do not acknowledge the necessity and rights of the law, then we regretfully must ignore it as well, becoming, as necessary, judge, jury and executioner.

While we believe we have identified the majority of Teragen members, we do not, as of yet, have a clear picture of the actual leadership or organization within the group. Few in the Directive believe the claims that there is no such governing body. While we know that many Teragen operate on their own, based entirely upon the written philosophies of Divis Mal and others, we also have clear evidence pointing to some sort of organizing force. What this force might be remains unknown. Some indications suggest that Divis Mal himself leads an inner cadre of Teragen. Whether or not this cabal simply proselytizes "the word" or actually directs illegal and destructive activity remains unknown. Other indications point to a schism within the group, with some leaning toward violence and others ostensibly supporting more peaceful actions. We have little evidence to convince us the latter group truly wants peace as we would define it.

The most interesting theory about the Teragen holds that the inner circle works in conjunction with Project Utopia. Could the public feud between the two groups be a front for a hidden alliance? Is the Teragen merely a way for Project Utopia to carry out patently illegal and destructive acts without sullying its good name? Some indications point to yes. There is substantial overlap between known Teragen members and novas who have registered with or otherwise participated in Project Utopia undertakings. These coincidental memberships are particularly high among novas who erupted early on, i.e., the most experienced novas on the planet. We have some evidence that Divis Mal himself might have had dealings with Project Utopia in its earliest stages. For now though, we have no solid proof of links between the two nova groups, but several operational and intelligence cells are devoted full-time to investigating the possibility.

AOR: The Teragen

DIRECTIVE FILE: EG 115
REL: PI, ES, MN, CL
IPSP: Critical
ENCRYPTION: Delta

No greater threat to baseline independence and peace of mind exists today. Just one of these beings has the potential to change the course of history within his own lifetime. By himself. No single man or woman in history has shown that capacity. If even one of these reports of mine was to get out to a nova with enough power and ambition, we could be hunted down (to a man) and removed with ease.

The Teragen organization is the ultimate expression of the threat novas represent. Some novas can be tamed and directed toward humanitarian ends; those of the Teragen cannot. Teragen novas have all but declared war on mankind.

Divis Mal

And what of this "Angel of Destruction" himself? With the one exception of his spectacular conflict with Caestus Pax in Bahrain in 2010, he has maintained a relatively low profile since the publication of his damned treatise. His detainment and interrogation are top priorities among Omega Division operatives. We must discover what sort of a mind is capable of writing *The Null Manifesto*. We must learn what sort of mind is capable of convincing hundreds of novas to cast off their very humanity and turn themselves into monsters. The novas of the Teragen may not follow Divis Mal (or he may not lead them), but they do listen to him. If we can get inside the head of the nova that the Teragen idolizes, we can discover a way to tear the organization apart from the inside.

The worst implication in Mal's remaining remote, however, is that he now offers no guidance to the Teragen. You all saw the riots that occurred when we put an end to the Newsman's influence; the supporters he had stirred up fell into chaos when their leader's voice became silent. They relied so much on the Newsman's words that they did not know what to do without it. The rioting only lasted for two days, but the Newsman's influence was relatively minor in comparison to Mal's. And the Newsman's influence applied almost exclusively to baseline citizens. Mal, however, has swayed powerful novas to his way of thinking. His writings even managed to convert Operative Hooks, and Hooks tested higher on the Mobile-Reliability Scale than the majority of our baseline operatives. In Mal's continued absence, what will his followers do? Divis Mal must be brought to heel before this situation gets out of hand.

Geryon

Geryon represents all that is ugly, brutish and terrifying about the Teragen. Some call him an enforcer to Divis Mal. Some call him the Teragen's avatar of destruction. Do not believe this rubbish, but do be aware that Geryon is one of the most dangerous Teragen-affiliated novas in existence. He has committed political murders in the name of his philosophy, with just the disregard for human life Mal wrote about. Worse, his attacks are not as much assassinations as back-alley-type physical assaults that baseline authorities are almost powerless to predict or prevent. The most confounding aspect of Geryon's method of attack is that he has perfected his ability to escape all observation and pursuit. Since the murder of Frederick Rupert, Omega Division agents have been assigned to bring Geryon down. However, our nova agents have not even been able to track him. I think an eight-foot-tall mass of muscle, scales and flesh would be easy to spot and capture, but one report by an Alpha Division team stated that in their pursuit of Geryon from the grounds of the United States Capitol, the suspect fled into a terrified, scattering crowd of tourists and somehow managed to completely evade detection thereafter. The agents in the field suspected some quantum power of invisibility or camouflage, but they could detect no quantum signature that would prove that guess correct. Our only remaining theory is that Geryon is able to shut down his quantum-channeling abilities much like our own nova operatives are trained to do, making him indistinguishable from any other baseline. I needn't explain how dangerous this ability makes this monster.

Raoul Orzaiz

Count Orzaiz sits on the reverse side of the Teragen coin. The danger he represents is that of the cunning serpent or devil. He doesn't say, "If you are the son of God, create food to feed yourself," he says, "Are you hungry? Here, have some bread. Don't thank me; just remember where you got it."

You requested estimative intelligence on Orzaiz' potential to be a Teragen defector and his viability as a Directive contact. There is none. Orzaiz is too assured of his own superiority to mankind to even consider an offer like that. At best, he would listen patiently, explain why you were wrong to approach him, offer you one of his many guest bedrooms for the evening, then offer you breakfast and see you to the door in the morning. At worst, the question would offend him, and you would find yourself the victim of Orzaiz' political scorn and the enmity of the entire Teragen.

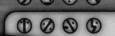

Interview Exerpt

Excerpt from an interview with Count Orzaiz for "America's Talking!," May 19, 2006
Reuben: "And are you worried about reprisals from the Directive?"
Orzaiz: "Who?"

I think this a good sign. In reality, I doubt the count is ignorant of our existence. More likely, he thinks so little of us that he doesn't think of us at all. Either way, not being considered a threat by a member of the Teragen is something to be proud of. There is, however, the possibility that he was simply being disingenuous....

Operation Turncoat failed, and any attempts to monitor the Teragen from the inside are likely to fail with similarly disastrous consequences. I recommend we determine potential targets for Teragen attacks, warn the appropriate agencies, develop Titan-class countermeasures and continue our surveillance of other known or suspected Teragen novas.

—Chancellor Erich Galt

AOR: Project Utopia

DIRECTIVE FILE: PI 098
REL: All division heads (File for inclusion with Sternych Missive)
IPSP: Standard
ENCRYPTION: Alpha

Every day, I see the word Utopia in some newspaper or OpNet headline. This day, it has single-handedly made the environment safe; the next, it has secured a deal with the United Nations; after that, it seeks to be the first organization to harness novas (like horses, yes) for space exploration. As an arrogant teenager, I read black-market copies of Orwell beneath my covers with a flashlight, and I see an all too familiar pattern in this Utopia's behavior. Who was *Animal Farm*'s Napoleon to oust the old farmers? Who was Big Brother to decide that "his" people needed watching over? Who is Justin Laragione of Project Utopia to make our tomorrow brighter for us? I may be the heretic of this new age, but I make no secret of asking this question.

No nova organization presents more of a conundrum to us than Project Utopia. Even if you take everything their propaganda says as truth (and we don't), the Directive would still have mixed feelings about the Aeon Society-founded organization. Ostensibly, it exists to help novas deal with their newfound abilities, to channel them toward constructive ends and to help the world at large. Indeed, the record shows that Utopia has done all of these things. More insidious, as far as

we are concerned, is the Project's not-quite-stated goal of serving as the public image booster for novas the world over. Although its leaders are quick to denounce violence and criminal behavior, they usually play such incidents down and emphasize the "good" that novas supposedly do every day.

Thus, Project Utopia works against our goal of raising public awareness as to the danger novas present. Utopia's skilled promotion and the wild popularity of Team Tomorrow prove that we have a long way to go before even the populations of our member nations see the true state of things, much less the world as a whole. That challenge alone would mark Utopia as an enemy of sorts, at least on the political front. Add into the mix the fact that Utopia keeps the most comprehensive list of novas on the planet, along with important medical and psychological data about every nova that comes through one of their many doors. That is information we need to have. Thus far, complete penetration of the Utopia computer network has eluded us, but the fragments we have seen prove just how vital it is that we see the whole picture. Once again, another reason for us to consider Utopia a foe to be dealt with.

We shall no doubt overcome these problems in time. The most significant threat Utopia presents is its ability to influence and even control large numbers of novas. Team Tomorrow on its own is a formidable force, although, fortunately, it thus far seems devoted to acts that do not jeopardize our security. Other Utopia teams around the world continue to perform deeds designed to increase the Project's prestige and bank accounts. With each passing year the strength, number and caliber of novas working directly for Utopia grows. Although the Project shows no definitive signs of threatening member-nation security, its threat potential has become staggering. Should Utopia ever seek to use its power and influence unethically, the world could suffer staggering consequences. Again, one more reason that Utopia belongs on our list of enemies, real or potential.

Breaking Apart From Within

Now for the conundrum. Not all novas exist under the sway of Project Utopia. Most particularly the Teragen (certain theories aside) seems adamantly opposed to the Project and its controlling practices. The Teragen danger is a known quantity, a fact no one with all the evidence at hand can

dispute. Any help Utopia can offer in beating back this terrorist, nova-supremacist movement is welcome, for the time being. After all, until our technological advances and nova-neutralization tactics catch up with the power level of current quantum powered threats, novas remain the best defense against other novas.

In an ideal world, the Teragen and Project Utopia would effectively wipe each other out or, at least, leave the victorious organization so crippled that we could move in for the kill with relative impunity. In fact, a number of Directive cells are currently exploring ways of making this dream come true, playing one side against the other as best they can. Fortunately, neither side needs much encouragement. The Directive has enjoyed early success in this program, and as our channels for disinformation grow, we expect even better results.

A more interesting case is the mysterious new group of novas calling themselves Aberrants. Although not much of a threat in and of themselves, the Aberrants raise an interesting question. They believe that Project Utopia has some sinister, secret plan for novas. Moreover, they believe this plan involves controlling novas, even on a genetic level. The Aberrants seem to have some good, but not decisive, evidence for their claims. If true, it may be that Project Utopia, or some sub-group within it, secretly wants much the same thing we do: control over the potential nova threat. In that case, destroying Utopia outright could actually be counterproductive. Perhaps we can deal with this secret cabal or, more likely, subvert it or co-opt for our own purposes. Either way, the possibility deserves more exploration. Discovering the truth behind these rumors has become a top priority.

No matter what our ultimate decision regarding Utopia's fate, for now our mission remains much the same: Infiltrate and monitor Project Utopia to the greatest extent possible. Placing loyal operatives within the Project continues to have high priority, as does compromising existing Utopia employees and converting them by hook or by crook to our cause. The success or failure of any such ongoing operations remains strictly confidential and is beyond the cope of this document. All cells, intelligence and operational, have standing orders to watch for potential areas of exploitation vis-à-vis the Project and its members.

Team Tomorrow

The shining heroes of Utopia's Team Tomorrow are the most exhilarating phenomenon since the earliest days of the KGB. Similarly, they are the proud defenders of an ideal, willing and able to do what the common man cannot in order to protect the ideals of its parent organization. Yet why then are those who were once so afraid of the KGB (or the NKVD or even our FSB) so willing to accept Team Tomorrow as their savior? True, the various teams around the world have made great strides in ensuring global peace. They have checked the progress of organized crime in all major theaters around the world, as well as filling in the role NATO's troops were once best suited to play. The Yaroslav Radocani situation, for example, displayed the thoroughness and professionalism with which Team Tomorrow units are trained to act. The strikes Team Tomorrow personnel have made against Camparelli-Zhukov operations make my former SOBRE comrades seem as ineffectual as night watchmen. Even our own agents are comforted by the notion that, when things get hairy, they can call upon Team Tomorrow. While I have disabused my own agents of that notion to the best of my ability, I fear that other Directive operatives (especially the Americans and Japanese who grew up on comic books and video games) are still taken with the idea that they can call on Team Tomorrow to save the day when they get themselves into trouble.

But, how can any of our agents look at Team Tomorrow's exploits without just as much fear as admiration? I once saw Caestus Pax break through the wall of a Zhukov cocaine factory like it was paper, stand serene in a hail of gunfire and the explosion of a grenade, then destroy both floors of the building, without breaking a sweat. He ended a two-week stalemate between the Mafia and the police by himself. And during standard operations, this man works with a team of equally powerful novas under the T2M banner. My agents have approached employees of the Team Tomorrow complex in Europe; each nova on the payroll is dedicated to Utopia to a fault. Imagine if Adolph Hitler had commanded such devoted superhumans. Divided front or not, this world would be dominated by the Reich, and none would be able to oppose its might. And yet, we rely on the professed good will of Project Utopia to "do what is best" for the entire world. If the Project's favor turns to malice or worldwide despotism with Team Tomorrow as its enforcer, who could stand against it? Are even *we* equipped to deal with such an eventuality?

The Aeon Society

To answer the above questions, I had to relocate a division of data analysts to the United States, for it is there that the Project was born. The ever-helpful open source records of the United Nations pointed out that Utopia was the offspring of a philanthropic organization known as the Aeon Society. Few records exist of the Aeon Society at the worldwide level, which implied that the organization had been born as a private enterprise. However, numerous UN records also show a long history of cooperation between those two organizations, leading back to the failed League of Nations. Perhaps the American Congress felt the

same way the Directive does, yes? Its resistance to joining that league might indicate a reluctance to cooperate with the Aeon Society that is similar to the Directive's suspicion of Project Utopia.

In any case, our research has proven both fruitful and disappointing. Examining the UN's records, we dug into early accounts of Aeon Society cooperation, following suspiciously quickly on the heels of the first public nova eruptions. Spokespersons for the Aeon Society offered their support to the UN in the catalogue and study of the nova phenomenon within just a month of Randel Portman's famous eruption. While the governments of the world struggled to understand what was happening and why people all over the world were changing, this society came to the fore remarkably fast.

Further prying uncovered the fact that Lawrence Quinn Jr., who helped prepare the preliminary draft of the Zurich Accord seemingly overnight, had a connection to the society as well. The executor of the estate from which Mr. Quinn inherited his considerable wealth also managed the estate of Dr. Richard Mercer. Dr. Mercer's estate generated the wealth from which his son, Maxwell Anderson Mercer, founded the Aeon Society. The connection may seem coincidental, but the attorney in ques-

tion, David Stephenson, served no other clients in the interim between when he worked for Dr. Mercer and Lawrence Quinn's grandfather. In fact, Mr. Stephenson apparently came out of retirement specifically to deal with the late Mr. Quinn's estate. We have yet to form definitive conclusions from this information, but the connection certainly bears further investigation. I recommend dispatching a cell of operatives to investigate the elderly Maxwell Anderson Mercer himself. If evidence exists that points to a more insidious relationship between the Aeon Society, Project Utopia and the United Nations than the friendly cooperation that we have witnessed, we would do well to discover it and expose it.

Even more disturbing is the fact that the Triton Foundation also nurtured its roots in the soil of the Aeon Society. As the foundation is another global organization set on doing good for all mankind, it parrots the aims of Project Utopia within the province of medical science. It works closely with Project Utopia, and it grew up out of the same organization that gave Project Utopia birth. The Aeon Society lies at the heart of both organizations, and as such, we must devote manpower and resources to the continued surveillance of it. However, if asked to rank its importance in terms of the Directives stated goals, I would rate it a low priority. For

now, the society's current brainchild, Project Utopia, should remain a top intelligence priority.

"The Conspiracy"

After the collection and analysis of a great deal of information, we have come to the conclusion that the so-called "Aberrants" have a valid complaint: There does seem to be some manner of conspiracy or secret faction within Project Utopia that does not uphold the same ideals as the group as a whole or those of Utopia's director. This secret faction maintains extreme protocols where secrecy and security are concerned, and the information we have been able to gather is extremely limited. Whether this faction is responsible for the death of Jennifer Landers or any other Utopian novas is difficult to ascertain, but we believe, based on limited evidence, that it is probable. In the interest of discerning the truth of the matter, we have recently requested that our Utopia-infiltration teams be trebled. If Project Utopia is harboring, fostering or creating criminals, it is best that the Directive, and possibly the public, be aware of it. Having more eyes on our target makes the Directive's job that much easier. The less willing the people of the world are to believe the first thing Project Utopia tells them, the more willing they become to accept the truth — whatever that truth happens to be.

—Director Ilyanovich

Aberrants

The so-called Aberrants represent a disaffected group of novas with a grudge against Project Utopia. They justifiably claim that Utopia has grown corrupt and that it plots to control novas for its own ends. We cannot argue with them on this point. The question for us is, what should we do about it? Any activity that weakens Utopia ought to be encouraged, that's the official line anyway. As long as the Aberrants activities remain focused against Utopia, we have no qualms about letting them fight one another. However, the Aberrants are, at their heart, a secret, revolutionary organization. We must keep a careful watch on them to make sure they do not venture into other fields that might harm the Directive's interests or those of humanity at large.

The Directive has positively identified 13 Aberrants inside and outside of Project Utopia. One of our operatives has discovered an excellent way to use this information to our advantage. Aberrants know they have much to fear should Project Utopia discover their true affiliation. We have, on several occasions, blackmailed Aberrants into serving our ends, rather than having us reveal their identities to Utopia. Although not a tool to be used lightly, it does give us an edge against the Project when and if we need it. Best of all, nei-

ther the Aberrants nor Utopia has any idea that we are behind the extortion.

AOR: The Aberrants

DIRECTIVE FILE: AH 041
REL: Cell leaders and analysts.
IPSP: Standard
ENCRYPTION: Beta

Let's get one thing straight between us at the top level so our agents aren't running around with false impressions, wasting our resources and putting themselves in danger: These "Aberrants" are not criminals. Since we can see the larger picture, we may be tempted to believe that their secretive actions and near-constant paranoia indicate guilt for some crime. However, it doesn't. Both suspected and professed Aberrants claim that they're in hiding and on the run from elements within Project Utopia. While I won't guess how right they are about some conspiracy within the Project (that's Petr's people's area of responsibility), I can tell that the Aberrants believe what they're preaching. They're on the run because they're scared, not because they're guilty of something.

I have assigned numerous cells of operatives to collect current intelligence on the Aberrants and to speak with the renegades themselves, in hopes of opening a dialogue. Taking into account how uneasy Project Utopia seems to get at the mention of the Aberrants, it is logical to conclude that the information those novas have somehow concerns the Project itself. Sure, the Aberrants have engaged in small-scale acts of terrorism against certain Utopian projects, but much less so than the Teragen or even religious zealots have. It's quite possible that the Aberrants are on to something. If we combine our intelligence with that being protected by the Aberrants, we can answer questions concerning Project Utopia that will put many enquiring minds at ease.

However, those Aberrants we can find and approach are more skittish than deer. They bolt at the first overt signs of surveillance, and they take extreme measures to avoid face-to-face contact with our field agents. To them, we seem "part of the machine," which remains detrimental to our objectives. I'm sure you all remember the incident in New York last month. Alpha Division operatives had arranged the collection opportunity of a suspected Aberrant informant in the twin towers of the World Trade Center. The operation proceeded smoothly until something spooked the informant and he leapt out the window, traveled *across* the intervening distance to the other tower, crashed

through the fire-safety window on the parallel floor and disappeared. None of the operatives were hurt, but we lost a potentially valuable information asset. That, team-leaders, is the most frustrating aspect of the Aberrant novas. They do not let us get close enough to make a reasonable assessment of their case and cause. We can't even make good stalking horses out of them.

As of yet, the Aberrants pose no direct threat to the security of the Directive's member nations, but I recommend viewing them with concern. They are powerful, outnumbered, scared and apparently in possession of information that could get them into a great deal of trouble. We must handle these novas with extreme caution. Else, we might never find out what they are hiding.

—Director Arnold Harris

AOR: Elites

DIRECTIVE FILE: MN 011
REL: PI, ES, EG, CL. Associated support staff. Released on request.
IPSP: Standard
ENCRYPTION: Alpha

As speculated, fellow Directive leaders, the coming of retainable novas was inevitable. Whether as a product of their own greed or that of innovative baseline opportunists, it was only a matter time before novas took it into their heads the idea that the whoring out of their quantum-generated abilities was imminently profitable. It stands to reason that the best goods and services are those for which the highest prices can be charged (and thus do they generate the greatest returns for their investors), and who better to provide said goods and services than beings who are themselves the "best"? Add to this tenet the fact that novas' superior abilities are so varied in their expression, and you realize that nova entrepreneurs and those entrepreneurs who exploit novas have the potential to become virtually unassailable economic forces. Boiled down to its essence, this factor is what propagates the tradition of nova elites, among both entrepreneurs and novas themselves.

Less surprising is the use of novas-for-hire by governments around the world. My own government typifies this inevitability in its *Saisho* initiative. Working from the preceding economic model, we decided that subsidizing nova-conducted technological research was the most worthwhile investment we could make against the efforts of beings superior to ourselves. While most governments have not adopted the same approach, many do employ novas in strictly military- or national-security-related roles. Despite the fact that only relying on novas in this shortsighted capacity is

foolhardy in the long run, no government can reasonably be expected *not* to do so.

Our observers and analysts (who are novas themselves, for a touch of irony) all concur that novas are more a deterrent in the world military arena than weapons of mass destruction. While it is perfectly logical to assume that a nova scientist could develop a bomb or bioengineered disease that is orders of magnitude more devastating than even today's nuclear weapons, it is an odd baseline tendency to fear the being capable of creating such a device rather than the device itself. In fact, the American witticism, "Guns don't kill people; people kill people," demonstrates this concept beautifully. The very presence of novas on your payroll is enough to give opposing countries pause. Therefore, the more novas your government employs in its own interests, the more intimidating an appearance it creates in global affairs. If called upon to speculate, I would offer that such thinking is what makes Project Utopia the target of paranoid slander on such a regular basis.

DeVries

The DeVries Agency is little more than an old, lucrative notion repackaged for the so-called "Nova Age." By offering the most powerful mercenaries money can buy to individuals and corporations with more money than ethical sense, DeVries has amassed quite a fortune. This agency has secured for itself the comfortable niche of being the first and foremost nova-employment agency on the planet. It caters both to novas looking for specialized work and to companies, individuals or even governments looking for novas with specialized capabilities. If you have the money and you desire the publicity, the DeVries Agency can place nova power at your disposal. By the same token, the DeVries Agency can place equally capable, less overt nova operatives in your hands for a substantially higher fee. DeVries elites have a reputation for being the best trained, most adaptable, most reliable and most discreet operators in the business. What's more, the agency owes no particular country allegiance, so its novas are unrestricted by national boundaries. The only ways to prevent a DeVries nova from accepting a project are not offering him enough money, incurring the agency's professional disdain or exploiting a contractual prohibition in your favor.

At the same time, DeVries employs one of the largest, most versatile forces of novas on the planet, notably larger than Team Tomorrow and my country's own Nippontai. As these novas' employers change so often, their loyalties most commonly lie with DeVries. Interviews with detained DeVries novas have yielded little in the way of actionable intelligence on fellow operatives within the agency, and the nondisclosure agreement they sign upon employment gives them ample reason to remain silent.

Directive efforts to inspect DeVries Agency personnel records have met with strict resistance. Operatives at all levels of authority have entered DeVries Agency offices all over the world demanding lists and descriptions of nova personnel on the payroll, all in the interests of national security and worldwide peace of mind. However, despite whatever authorization we display, the agency remains intractable. It defends the confidentiality of its agents and its records with a cadre of attorneys that boasts a sub-section of progressivist nova lawyers. By setting legal precedents in world courts, this team writes as much commercial and privacy law as it needs to ensure the agency's invulnerability to our scrutiny. If DeVries remains uncooperative, I recommend approaching the Security Council of the United Nations and demanding satisfaction. Such a measure will certainly alert Project Utopia to our aims, but most likely, the Utopians are just as curious as we are about who the DeVries Agency keeps secret.

Should this initiative fail, I have detailed a plan for the clandestine collection of the records in question. I recommend preparing the listed Beta and Omega Division operatives in File: MN 011-A as my representatives approach the Security Council. Thus, we can be in position to initiate the operation immediately if the Security Council proves unhelpful.

—M.N.

Others

I can provide you with more upon request (see the attached files), but the task of "collecting intelligence on unaligned elements of the Nova Age with bearing on international interests" is little more than asking me to predict not only where your errant needle is, but in which haystack and on what farm. *Every* nova has the potential to affect the entire world, gentlemen, and it's useless to speculate on how each one will attempt to do so. An independent party of novas has been lobbying the UN in an attempt to cut short the proposed Antarctic Terraforming Project. Have they discovered some side effect to the terraforming process that would melt the polar ice continent and flood the world? Are they secretly building their own base there from which to launch an offensive against the rest of the world? I imagine the Protectors would take umbrage at that, but no one can say. I recommend realigning one of our reconnaissance satellites to scan the continent, but I cannot justify the diversion of that resource away from any other collection initiative.

Independent SIGINT sonar readings confirm that something gargantuan either moved or exploded less than 100 miles off the coast of Talaud Island, but none of our countries' combined naval forces can offer a plausible

explanation. The residual traces of quantum energy our nova agents detected give us some clue, but it doesn't lead anywhere. Is Leviathan rising? Did a diseased nova go there to die? We have no way to know.

I have seen Alejandra perform, I watched Corbin play his last soccer game, and I remember reading the Newsman's editorials. Every one of those novas has the power to sway me, just as they did the thousands of other unsuspecting people present to see and hear them. How can we deal with a phenomenon of this magnitude? Here's the answer to that, gentlemen: Individuals cannot. The Directive as a group, however, must rise to the occasion.

My primary objective in writing this file (other than to lambaste those who would seek to fritter away MI6 funds by trying to make us run in circles) is to illustrate how futile a small-time approach is to accomplishing our goals. We cannot anticipate how novas will change us or how they will affect the world. We must, instead, be proactive and vigilant. As part of this new vigilance, it would behoove us to meet to discuss which independent novas top our list of potential threats. Then, we will analyze these individuals and ascertain the level of threat they present to our interests and decide what to do about it. Quite frankly, however, we have more than enough to do just keeping abreast of the dealings of Project Utopia, the dominant criminal cartels that survive Utopia's wrath, the Aberrant movement, the Teragen and the elite phenomenon.

—Lathrop

The Protectors

We've no idea what to make of the Protectors. A group of novas that wishes to exile itself to the inhospitable wastes of Antarctica seems, on the face of things, to present very little threat. According to their own statements, the Protector's members simply wish to be left alone. Unfortunately, we cannot necessarily believe their statements, and we are left wondering if they may have a certain survivalist or militia mindset that could become problematic later. Although they have not, as of yet, done anything to warrant extreme suspicion, their very isolationist nature renders them suspicious. After all, having moved to the southernmost continent, they have effectively removed themselves from the community of nations, and no government has authority over them. An attempt by them to set up a nova free state could have far-reaching and undesirable consequences. Furthermore, their remote location makes it extremely difficult to monitor their activities. We have no contacts or sources in their ranks. For now, the Protectors remain a low priority target, but we must remain vigilant toward the south. Eventually, the group will have to be dealt with.

AOR: Unaligned Novas

DIRECTIVE FILE: CL 004
REL: [Open Source Information Enclosed]
IPSP: Standard
ENCRYPTION: Alpha

Beyond the issue of organized nova groups lie the more complicated issues associated with individual novas who, of their own volition, present a real threat. In most cases these are men and women who, before their eruption, already leaned toward dangerous beliefs of some kind. Textbook examples include Gary Wilson and his Free State militia in the United States, a single nova who was already a radical right-wing extremist even before he came into his quantum powers. Distrustful of all but his fellow militia members, he refused to join any established nova group. However, he used his powers and followers to launch a series of domestic terrorist attacks, attacks that no one could legally convict him of thanks to his nova abilities. The Directive managed to handle the situation and neutralize the threat, but there are dozens more like Wilson around the world that we must contend with in the present and in the future.

I've voiced my disregard for this medium on numerous occasions, so I won't belabor you with the same speech. Attached, you'll find a sample of the actionable intelligence we've gathered on one of the world's most influential unaligned novas.

(Point of note: King William was not amused by the diversion of MI6's resources to the Fitz-Novas of the new age. Next time we assign areas of responsibility, I recommend a drawing of lots.)

Anibál Buendia

The eufiber magnate from Costa Rica doesn't even do anything, and yet, he's one of the most sought-after social figures of our time. How does one handle that? How would you take it if every chap from New York to Milan to Calcutta to Tokyo was after you for the white mess that popped from your acne spots? We've made this lazy beachcomber famous, but what do we know about this *materia regia*? Before we banned its use, we saw our own agents attune eufiber to themselves, and it responded to their slightest mental suggestion. Buendia controls the colonies still attached to him like prehensile hair. What's more, the substance demonstrates a capacity to store quantum radiation. We haven't even begun investigations into what effect that property has on baseline consumers who wear or use eufiber products. The synthetic alternative is all well

and good, but there's an awful lot of the actual material. It's all the rage in *haute couture* circles and it has trickled down into mainstream culture. It now pervades almost every world society at some level.

This is, and should continue to be, a matter of concern to the Directive. There is still far too much we don't know about eufiber. For instance, why doesn't it "die" when it's detached from Buendia? Why does it transmit some types of energy like a conductor but store others like a capacitor? Nova capabilities are all, in some way, related to the circumstances surrounding the nova's eruption and the personality of the nova in question. What kind of circumstances and what kind of man can give birth to the bizarre substance now called eufiber? What does it take to make a spotty Costa Rican one of the most valuable worldwide assets of our time?

[BEGIN DIRECTIVE COMMUNIQUÉ]
Top Secret

[DIRECTIVE FILE]
Encryption Code: Malachi-7-12
Date: July 25, 2008
To: J. Yarbrough, Director — Media Relations
From: S. Park, Field Monitor
Subject: The View from Without

Director Yarbrough:

As per your instructions, here is my preliminary report. I have been searching through the OpNet, looking for references to our organization, both veiled and overt, and examining our public perception. Though this report is far from complete, the information contained within is the most current and relevant that I have found thus far. And it seems our suspicions have been confirmed.

Of the sites I have searched, most people believe just what we want them to believe: The Directive is a multinational intelligence agency that is not very good at what it does. But beyond that, the results vary dramatically.

The Official Site of The Directive

Welcome to the Directive's home on the OpNet! We're glad you came to find out more about us. We are a multinational peacekeeping force designed to help the many governments of the world work with Novas to keep things running smoothly for everyone.

- **About the Directive**
- **What's New at the Directive**
- **Publications**
- **Frequently Asked Questions**
- **Vision, Mission and Values of the Directive**
- **Related Links**
- **Employment**

Employees of the Directive enjoy many benefits, not the least of which is the opportunity to see the world! To find out more about the perks our employees have, just choose one of the individual titles below:

- **Comprehensive Health Plan**
- **Child Care**
- **Annual Paid Vacations**
- **Travel Stipend**
- **Advancement Opportunities**

Mr. Director, I am sure you are familiar with our OpNet site. It tells what we want everyone to know and does its best to hide what really goes on. Plain, vanilla and exactly what is expected. Through it, we maintain our public face and give the curious access to our public files.

Espionage from A to Z

Spies and Secrets, the OpNet site for Junior Secret Agents

The Directive – a UN-sanctioned
     information gathering organization
     helping world governments deal
     with novas.

- What the Directive is and what it does
- Mission Statement of the Directive
- The Directive's World Factbook
- What is Intelligence?
- The Directive's Chain of Command
- Why can't I find out more?

For more information, choose here to go to
THE DIRECTIVE's OpNet site.

This area is UNDER CONSTRUCTION. Please watch your step in this department.

Their Eyes Are Upon You

Excerpt from "Schadenfreude" follows, translated from the German:

"And what if I told you that on this night, the same night that Slider was killed, on a highway not 60 miles away, a large military-type truck was stopped by a police officer. And what was this truck carrying? No one knows. The officer's report is blank, and the truck was allowed to go on about its clandestine business. And why should this concern us? Certainly they don't want it to concern us. Just a routine traffic stop on a most evil of evenings, right? But this officer wasn't alone. Oh, no. He was training someone, a young recruit on one of his first patrols. And what did he say? This young soul claimed that when the truck was searched, the back was full of soldiers all wearing blue uniforms and berets! But his partner, his teacher, his mentor, after being taken aside by the driver, allowed them to pass and apologized for the inconvenience! Apologized! For delaying Slider's assassins from their deadly business! And what happened to this brave soul who came to us with this tale? Disappeared. The Directive cleaning up its messes."

Ms. Trepper is right on here. Another recent spotting of these "men in blue" comes in from Kenya, where one of our spotters saw them helping out with an inoculation by the Red Cross. When he asked why they were there, he was told they were safeguarding the volunteers and medical supplies from bandits. We know better. The Directive was there implanting the Mark of the Beast project that we have been talking about: small transmitters individually tuned so they can track us from space. They are similar to the ones they place in pets, but more sophisticated. Luckily, they are still in the testing stage and in isolated areas, but who knows when Kansas will seem isolated enough for them? For more information, see the **MOVING TARGETS** site for a full report.

Are novas safe? A new report from one of our scientist spotters speculates about the safety of eufiber. He states that if all these clothes are grown from a nova, who is to say that this same nova can't control them from a distance, like some who can disengage parts of their bodies and send them out. What if this same nova one day decides to paralyze or strangle everyone wearing eufiber? Frightening stuff, man. Check it out at the **GROWING CONCERN** area.

This is where things get troublesome. These so-called "spotters" are a very large group. They have eyes all over the world and manage to see a fair amount of things that many agencies, including ours, don't want seen. Luckily, they are still a fractious group and, for the most part, have no idea what they have seen when they do witness something. As long as we can keep them distracted with as many false movements as real maneuvers, they will not be a threat. And as for the truck full of agents, my reports indicate they were a group of United Nations Security Force troops on the way to the airport. But I am sure you already knew that.

GeoPol, The Global Political Discussion Site

The Clandestine Chat Area

MaKeoVel: And who exactly does this Directive answer to? The United Nations? NATO? The Confederation? Or to whomever has the deepest pockets?

Man-Tizz: Not my point, fella. What I meant was, why do we need them? We have the FBI for at home, the CIA for away and the NSA to watch what people are saying to each other. Roosevelt warned against getting involved with global organizations and European problems, and the Directive is both.

Saxa: Wilson.

Man-Tizz: ????

Saxa: It was Woodrow Wilson who advised the US not to get involved. Check your history before spouting off, dumb-ass.

TRnT: Is dumb-ass supposed to be hyphenated?

BottmLne: The trouble I have is one of investment. We have invested... how much is it now? Or is the amount Top Secret as well? And what do we have to show for it. Zilch, as far as I can see.

Saxa: The only time we knew what the CIA was working on was when a dictator was killed or when a bunch of our guys got caught. Is that the sort of proof you are looking for Banker-man?

TRnT: Again with the hyphens. Abuse the privilege, and it will be taken from you.

> This is a good example of the usual fare on the myriad of chat areas around the OpNet. A lot of people with a little information and no manners stomping around making broad statements they can't back. Every once in a while, someone stumbles onto something, but we keep the junior officers prowling the sites looking for certain key phrases. Between them and our code breakers watching for patterns of writing that could be messages passing between agents, ours or theirs, these areas are fairly secure.

World Forum

Transcript from 8/13/05 interview with John A. Gordon, former Deputy Director of the CIA

Phipps: "And what about these new boys on the block, the Directive?"

Gordon: "First, the UN wants an army, and we say 'Fine, give 'em an army.' And we do. The real military secures the area first, then this token force moves in and never has to get its uniforms dirty. And now they want their own intelligence agency. Sure. I wonder if their spies have to wear those pretty blue berets, too."

Phipps: "So, it's safe to say, you don't think much of them?"

Gordon: "Listen, it's just another case of amateurs stumbling into a playing field with no idea what the rules are. Hell, these boys don't even know what sport is being played."

> And so we hear from yet another of our supporters. I am still getting the details of Gordon's departure from the Agency, but from the amount of difficulty I am having in acquiring anything more than rumor, it is safe to say it was not under the best of circumstances. All I have found so far, is that it had to do with a Directive led operation that was mishandled from the CIA end. I don't like to speculate, but from his statements, perhaps Gordon was the fall guy for this. I will let you know more as I discover it. Meanwhile, in his condemnation of all things intelligence related and in our group especially, he has reinforced our image even more: We are not important and should be ignored.

SCENE FROM THE MOTION PICTURE *BLOOD AND BLUE*

DANA: "PLEASE, DON'T HIT ME AGAIN! I DON'T KNOW ANYTHING, I SWEAR!"

THE MAN IN THE SUIT MOVES AROUND OUT OF THE DARKNESS, PAST THE ROW OF GLITTERING TORTURE IMPLEMENTS HE HAS LAID OUT NEXT TO THE CHAIR.

STRAUSS: "WE KNOW YOU ARE LYING, BUT I CAN'T UNDERSTAND WHY. YOUR HERO IS DEAD AND WON'T BE COMING TO SAVE YOU."

STRAUSS: "WE KNOW THAT YOU HAVE THE CHIP. WE WANT TO KNOW WHERE YOU HAVE HIDDEN IT. TELL US, OR WE WILL MAKE YOUR PAIN LAST FOR DAYS."

DANA: "I DON'T KNOW WHAT YOU'RE TALKING ABOUT! I NEVER GOT ANY CHIP. I TELLING YOU, YOU HAVE THE WRONG PERSON!"

STRAUSS CONFERS WITH THE OTHER MEN IN THE ROOM, STILL IN SHADOW.

STRAUSS: "VERY WELL MS. HOLTEN. IF YOU DO NOT HAVE THE INFORMATION WE SEEK, THEN IT IS POINTLESS TO WASTE MY TIME WITH TORTURE."

DANA RELAXES IN THE CHAIR, RELIEVED.

STRAUSS: "BUT AS YOU HAVE SEEN SO MUCH OF OUR ORGANIZATION, YOU CANNOT BE ALLOWED TO LIVE AND TELL OTHERS WHAT YOU KNOW."
DANA: "NO, I WON'T TELL ANYONE! I HAVEN'T SEEN ANYTHING!"
STRAUSS: "SHHH."
STRAUSS POINTS A SILENCED PISTOL AT HER HEAD.

STRAUSS: "THE DIRECTIVE MUST KEEP ITS SECRETS."

AT THAT MOMENT, THE DOOR BURSTS IN, AND BLAKE HARPER COMES IN BLASTING.

HE ROLLS INTO THE ROOM AND MANAGES TO HIT ALL THE MEN EXCEPT STRAUSS, WHO HAS TAKEN COVER BEHIND A METAL TABLE.

BLAKE: "THANK GOD, YOU ARE STILL ALIVE DANA!"

DANA: "I KNEW YOU WOULD COME FOR ME!"
BLAKE: "BUT WHERE IS STRAUSS?"

STRAUSS RISES FROM BEHIND THE TABLE, RIPPLING WITH PURPLE ENERGY.

BLAKE: "GREAT SCOTT! HE'S A NOVA!"

It just gets worse from there. I admit I included this as a bit of a joke. In monitoring the material that comes out of Hollywood and Mumbai, I have seen many depictions of the Directive agent. They run the gamut, but the majority is like this — vile über-patriots willing to kill to keep their secrets. The rest are usually bumbling idiots who have no idea how to survive on the streets and must be shown the way the real world works by a street-smart, hip, urban cop. The remainder are just as forgettable.

E-mail from Dramatic Designs
To: Thomas Vietch
Fr: John Tweeddale, Marketing Manager
Re: your suggestions
Mr. Vietch,
Let me preface my letter by saying how much I admire your work. Your sculpts on The Elites: At War! series were magnificent. Thanks to your quality work, we were able to move the line into production a full month ahead of schedule. None of that sending faulty work back to be redone. And for that, you have our gratitude.

But I am writing this in response to your e-mail last week, specifically in regard to your suggestions. While we respect your opinions and value your creativity, I don't think your ideas and ours are moving in the same direction. The idea for a line of Directive action figures is not without merit but would be difficult to create and maintain. They don't have cartoons or comics coming out to support the line. And the idea of 10 identically dressed figures with varying accessories is so early 90s. I think we have already learned our lesson on taking one figure and dressing him up in 20 different costumes. No one wants 20 variations of one guy! I respect your drive and your desire to move things ahead in our business, but we have teams of analysts and go-to people to decide what figures we need to be making. But keep up the good work! You're going to love what we have for you next.

Thanks again,
John

Apparently we are not marketable either.

This is just a small sample of the information that has come into my department since our inception. As you can tell, we are seldom thought of highly if we are thought of at all. It seems as if our resident spin doctors have been doing their job in keeping us out of sight and mind of the population.

And on a separate subject, it has come to my attention that Operation: SNAFU is in second stage. I know it is not technically in my area, but news does travel down the hall occasionally. I wish to register my opposition to this plan. The current situation, as I have shown, is either of ignorance or underestimation. The staging of a major failure will turn more eyes on us than we really want. My opinion is that we save such a plan for when we have become more visible and have more attention focused on us. This way we can divert the focus, by showing them we are not worth dedicated interest. But this is just my opinion, and I hope I haven't overstepped my bounds.

My full report will be ready in two weeks. I look forward to hearing back from you with your notes at your earliest convenience.

S. Park
Field Monitor

[END COMMUNIQUÉ]

Archive: Phone Intercept, March 18, 2007
Subject: Torture of Agent Martin Fuller
Speaker A: Teragen Terrorist Cornelius White
Speaker B: Unidentified

Cornelius White: What's up man?

Speaker B: Report.

CW: You'll never believe who I've got here.

B: Who?

CW: C'mon, guess.

B: I'm not going to play your games Cornelius.

CW: Ok, fine. Be that way.

B: Report. Now.

CW: I have, right here with me, one Martin Fuller.

B: And who is Martin Fuller.

CW: You know him better as Joshua Ballantrae. Turns out, there is no such person. Martin here has been playing a little game with us for the past three months.

B: Explain.

CW: Well, I had Mimi over for the weekend. She and Josh— I mean Martin, and I had a little party. Martin got a little loaded and started asking Mimi a lot of questions. Where was she from, what was her eruption like, what did she think about Utopia. Crap like that. Nothing too weird about it. Mimi though, she kind of liked the guy and so, well, you know how she is, she wanted to see what he was really after. She and I both thought he was just trying to get into her pants. So anyway, Mimi did her thing.

B: She scanned him?

CW: Yeah, she scanned him.

B: And she discovered his name was really Martin Fuller.

CW: No, that's the thing. She didn't get anything. She got nursery rhymes and math equations. She got old show tunes. She didn't get any surface thoughts and couldn't go deep at all.

B: He has some sort of psychic shield?

CW: No, Mimi says it wasn't a q-power. They guy was using mind games to block her out. Strange thing is, he didn't even seem to be trying, it was, like, built in to his brain. That's how she put it.

B: Interesting.

CW: So she tells me about this, and I decide to do a little digging into his personal effects while Mimi keeps him busy. I called the Hare over to help me out. The Hare went through this guy's stuff with a fine-tooth comb. Pulled out three transceivers and a bug from the lining of the guy's clothes (which he wasn't using at the time, thanks to Mimi).

B: He was bugged! How did you miss this?

CW: This was state-of-the-art stuff. Never seen anything like it.

B: We'll discuss it later. Go on.

CW: So the Hare and I decided to work him over a bit with Mimi's help. We grabbed the guy and got out of there, figuring our location was already compromised by the locators in his clothes. Sure enough we picked up a tail as soon as we left the hotel, but I lost it. Then we ended up here with nothing but time on our hands and a few questions.

B: You're in a secure location?

CW: Definitely. This is a coded phone, fresh line, and we swept the place clean before we got started. We've been here for about an hour. Turns out Martin isn't so tough after all. First we let Mimi have a crack at him. She gave it all she had. Kept tellin' this guy that she was gonna rape his mind and stuff like that. Well, whatever this guy's got goin' for him, he managed to wear her out. Then me and the Hare stepped in. He might have a tough mind but he sure doesn't like having his fingernails torn out with pliers. Doesn't like losing his teeth one at a time much either.

B: Few people would.

CW: He held out as long as he could, but I think Mimi wore him down for us. He certainly wore her down, she's passed out on the couch.

B: So you discovered that this man's real name is Martin something?

CW: Yeah, Martin Fuller, and he's a government agent. Says he works for the FBI. Says they've been watching the three of us for months, working with Project Utopia.

B: And you believe him.

CW: Well, it makes sense to me. Explains the bugs and the tail. The Hare isn't so sure though. He thinks the guy's still holding back. We're going to work him over again in a few minutes. I just wanted to call and check in and tell you what's up. We need to sterilize anything Joshua slash Martin ever had anything to do with.

B: I'll make the calls.

Noise: <smashing of a door, shouts>

CW: Damn, it's the Feebs!

Voice: Down! Down! Down! Down! Down!

Noise: <explosion, identified as stun grenade>

Noise: <gunfire, identified as Directive-issued weapons> <end transmission>

Follow-up Report: Agent Fuller was recovered alive and intact. He did not compromise any other agents involved in his cell nor did he reveal the Directive's involvement in the operation. Speaker B remain unidentified and unaccounted for.

CHAPTER FOUR: CLASSIFIED INFORMATION

Part One: New Backgrounds and Abilities

The Directive's greatest weapon in the struggle to keep the nova threat under control is their organization. Directive operatives can rely on an established intelligence network to support them whenever they need it. The following Background options reflect that support and are available only to Directive members (although characters from similar intelligence organizations might have the equivalent Backgrounds associated with their own group at the Storyteller's discretion). The Directive's cell structure makes having these backgrounds a key to individual success. They each represent influence within the organization and the ability to use its resources more effectively to carry out missions. Those resources are not unlimited, and as in any bureaucratic organization, those who know how to use the system prosper over those who do not.

Equipment

The Directive hopes to even the odds against novas through advanced technology. Although it's not there yet, Kuro-Tek (which effectively serves as the Directive's research and development arm) continues to produce new and exciting equipment for use in the intelligence field in general and designed specifically for use against novas. The Directive is not shy about buying the latest technology from other sources as well. With the United States, Germany and Japan being Directive member nations, the sponsoring organization has access to the latest in military, computer and high technology. While Project Utopia's Science and Technology Division still maintains a significant advantage over the Directive thanks to its monitoring of all new and developing technologies worldwide, the Directive is not without its own wellspring of formidable devices.

Getting that equipment out into the field for actual use is another matter. The Directive's funds are not unlimited, and it has set some pretty rigorous rules about who gets what and when. The Equipment background represents the character's connections and influence within the line of distribution. The more dots a charac-

Kuro-Tek

One of the foremost proponents of Japan's *Saisho* movement is a highly advanced research and development firm largely owned, operated and protected by the Nakato gumi and called Kuro-Tek. Project Utopia's Science and Technology division has officially declared Kuro-Tek enemy number one for their constant and seemingly unstoppable trafficking in contraband technology. The Directive, however, thanks to Japan's enthusiastic (if highly secretive) support of Kuro-Tek, enjoys the favors of this shadowy corporation. Kuro-Tek provides the Directive with devastating new equipment in exchange for a moderate fee and intelligence on Utopia's operations in Japan.

What Project Utopia's reaction might be if and when it should ever discover this alliance can only be speculated upon, but such a discovery would certainly do nothing to warm the relationship between Utopia and the Directive.

ter has, the more equipment he generally has at his disposal. The dots represent two different things simultaneously. First and foremost they measure the "level" of equipment available to the character. The more dots, the more expensive and/or experimental the equipment is the agent can lay his hands on.

The following chart describes the five different levels and the equipment associated with them. During the course of play, if the character needs a new piece of equipment he rolls a number of dice equal to his Manipulation + Equipment Background. He must get a number of successes equal to the level of equipment he needs (yes, it's still hard to get those tanks and planes). In general, a character can request a specific piece of equipment only once every week, although the Storyteller has ultimate discretion in this. Remember that if the Directive sees a glaringly obvious need for the character to have some item, the organization gives it to him if it can, but this usually only happens in the most obvious or dire of circumstances.

A character's Equipment level also determines the number of special items he starts play with. Each dot represents one item-level. If the character wants a level two item it costs two dots, a level three item costs three dots and so on. No character can have more than five dots in Equipment without first having worked his or her Backing up to six over the course of a series.

X Even a character without the Equipment Background can get these items at will: small arms, body armor, basic bugs and hidden microphones, video cameras and other common items one could buy at a store or find issued to police and security forces.

• Advanced bugs and hidden microphones that are difficult to detect, micro-cameras, machine-guns and other non-explosive heavy weapons.

•• High-level interrogation equipment such as portable lie detectors, brain-wave scanners and other delicate electronic equipment. Also hand-held rocket launchers and plastic explosives.

••• Experimental personal equipment like mental noise generators, node inhibiting drugs and other dangerous drugs and chemicals. Also armored (but not armed) vehicles and standard aircraft.

•••• Experimental weaponry such as EMP guns, portable laser weapons and other dangerous items. Also, control over orbiting spy satellites for a certain period of time (usually a week). Light military vehicles such as armored personal carriers and helicopters. Eclipsidol *may* be available to characters with this Equipment rating.

••••• The big stuff. Use of a nuclear submarine (but not the nukes), tanks, military jets and helicopters, access to space programs and shuttle launches.

Favors

While the Directive's administration and bureaucratic system exists to help the operatives work smoothly together and jointly achieve the organization's goals, the fact is that interpersonal relationships end up determining what actually gets accomplished. Like with any other group, there are rivalries and friendships within the Directive's ranks. The Favors Background represents the accumulated friendships and partnerships the character has made within the Directive. Calling upon these relationships allows the character to circumvent the usually tight Directive security and hierarchy. While this usually means violating rules concerning interaction between cells, sometimes it is the only way to get things done.

Dots in favors do not represent particular "favors" that others owe the character. Rather, they are an abstract measurement of how well connected the character is within the Directive. Note that connections and rank or position do not go hand in hand. The lowliest operative can be better connected than a high-ranking official if she has friends throughout the organization. Each time a character wishes to call in a favor, the player uses the Favors attribute just like it was a regular Ability. The Storyteller determines how difficult it is to get what the player wants and sets the minimum number of successes. The character then rolls Charisma + Favors to determine whether or not she succeeds.

A botched roll means that the character has burned up one or more contacts and loses a dot of Favors permanently. If they seem warranted, the Storyteller can give out additional dots in Favors at his or her discre-

tion, but they cannot be purchased with experience points.

X Getting a phone number or license plate traced.

• Getting information from another, low-ranking cell.

•• Getting information from an equal- or higher-ranking cell. Getting operational help from a lower ranking cell.

••• Getting information from the administrative or R&D level. Getting operational help from an equal or higher ranking cell.

•••• Getting information about operational plans of other cells. Getting operational assistance from the administrative level.

••••• Finding out some hints about the Directive's overall operations. Getting authority to command a number of different cells and resources for a short period.

Rank

The Directive has its own rank system, although not a clear hierarchy like one finds in traditional military units. Rank is a function of the operative's experience and reputation, the importance of her current assignment and the number of operatives under her command. This last quantifier presents the easiest way to compare ranks within the Directive. An individual commanding a major cell and several sub-cells "outranks" someone who heads a single, smaller cell. However, the former has no authority over the latter, merely more influence with, and importance in, the eyes of the administration.

Rank allows the character to issue orders to subordinates. In this, it is similar to the Followers background. The important difference is that the character has rank over her subordinates and can order them to perform any function within their job description. Another difference is that the character herself is part of that rank system and must answer to her superiors if she acts inappropriately or fails. Furthermore, her own subordinates will not obey orders they consider illegal or suicidal.

X A member of an intelligence or operational cell with no responsibilities beyond herself.

• Second in command within a cell, usually chosen to lead mission teams or intel task forces while the leader directs and coordinates the cell as a whole.

•• Leader of a minor cell with three to five operatives under her command.

••• Leader of a large cell with six to 10 operatives under her command.

•••• Leader of a major cell with two or more sub-cells, totaling as many as 20 or 30 operatives.

••••• A low ranking member of the administration, directing a number of cells and having some small say in overall Directive policy and vision.

Abilities

The Directive trains its operatives with the latest tradecraft in the intelligence community, giving them the skills they need to succeed against novas. Some of these techniques, such as resisting telepathic interrogation, are not available outside the Directive's training halls.

Analysis (Intelligence): Intel operatives sift through reams of data every day, looking for trends or indicators to help them better understand novas' actions and psyches. Your character can use this skill to process large amounts of data and draw conclusions about people's behavior patterns, personal habits and psyches and other valuable information.

Specialties: Financial Records, Image Analysis, Audio Recordings, Psychological Profiles

Shadowing (Wits): The ability to follow a target, especially a nova target, without being detected is an invaluable skill. Your character knows all the ins and outs of following someone without being seen. This skill is typically used by several agents in tandem, making it all the more difficult for the target to realize he's being tailed.

Thought Discipline (Special): The threat of telepathic interrogation by novas drove the Directive to develop a special training program for its operatives. Your character can blank his or her thoughts, putting up a screen against telepathic probes. This is a difficult skill to master and, unfortunately, has no other applications. There is no Attribute associated with the skill. Rather, each level in this ability subtracts one success from telepathic scans directed at the character. A character can never have a Thought Discipline rating higher than his or her Willpower. The maximum is still five, even if the character's Willpower exceeds this level.

Tradecraft (Intelligence): There are certain skills and tricks of the trade that only intelligence operatives know. These come under the general heading of Tradecraft, or the art of spying. Your character knows how to place and search for bugs, hidden cameras, wiretaps and other hidden intelligence gathering devices. You are also skilled at entering a room, searching it thoroughly and leaving no trace that you've ever been there. Additionally, you know all the ins and outs of spycraft, from dead letter drops and codes, to conducting surveillance through satellite imagery and using computer and paper records to do detailed background checks. Finally, this broad skill teaches your character the basics of film development and hidden photography.

Specialties: Codes, Long Distance Observation, Street Walking, Traffic

Part Two: Technology

The Directive has at its disposal not only the latest high-tech gadgetry from the world of intelligence, but the backing of Japan's Kuro-Tek and a number of their own inventions as well. The administration distributes technology as it sees fit to the various cells, trying to make sure everyone has what they need. Characters with the Equipment background have access to more technology than most because of their strong contacts or good reputation.

None of these items are for sale on the open market. Only national governments and certain very powerful private corporations and organizations can buy them. The only way to get a hold of them is to have them issued to you, steal them or purchase them on the black market.

Devices
CompReader

In the modern age, most organizations and security-sensitive individuals know better than to keep anything secret on a computer that's linked to the outside world, with its hackers and techno-spies. The Directive developed a device to get information from these isolated machines. The CompReader works by monitoring the electromagnetic fluctuations of a computer. The device picks up changes in the monitor and interaction with mouse and keyboard and sends that information to the CompReader, which then decodes the data and translates it onto its own screen. Thus, a person using the CompReader sees what the target computer displays in real time and records it all in the CompReader's memory.

An unshielded computer broadcasts such information up to 100 yards away. Shielded computers don't broadcast it beyond a few feet. The CompReader has several accessories to help crack shielded machines. A small transmitter, about one centimeter cubed, records all of the screen signals and can broadcast them to a CompReader within two kilometers. Alternatively, if signal security is an issue, the transmitter can simply record and then send out a burst transmission or wait for the owner to collect it. Such transmitters can also be used in relay to extend the CompReader's range, for both shielded and unshielded machines.

Eclipsidol

Description: Eclipsidol is a synthetic neurotransmitter that briefly sends a nova's M-R node into seizure.

Vector: Nearly any. Early forms of eclipsidol were all intramuscular, and those versions are still the easiest to come by, relatively speaking, but after Kuro-Tek realized that a significant percentage of novas were too tough or armored to be pierced by even the sharpest darts, Kuro-tek scientists made it deliverable by a variety of means. There are now contact, ingested and inhaled versions of eclipsidol.

Effect: Eclipsidol causes effected novas to instantaneously and uncontrollably shunt all of their quantum by any means possible, often to spectacular effect: Shapeshifting novas go through wild series of bizarre transformations, energy-channeling novas fire energy beams, bolts and barrages in all directions, flying novas zoom off in random directions or out into space, etc. A nova's power is wildly out of control for up to 30 seconds, followed by a span of up to five minutes during which the nova is wholly unable to manipulate quantum. All quantum powers, including Mega-Attribute enhancements, are disabled.

Mega-Attributes themselves are halved (round down) for the duration of the eclipsidol's effect.

Protection: Eclipsidol binds to neuroreceptors in the M-R node. If a nova thinks she may be dosed with eclipsidol (and has the proper contacts and sufficient resources), she can take an eclipsidol antagonist tablet to block eclipsidol intake for three to five hours. Very few individuals know of the existence of eclipsidol, and fewer still know that there's a way of avoiding its effects. Counter-eclipsidol tablets are extremely rare and issued only to the Directive's few nova agents. If they were available on the black market, counter-eclipsidol tablets would be *extremely* expensive, even for wealthy novas.

Antidote: Prevention is the only way of dealing with eclipsidol. There is no antidote, but the effects last only two to five minutes, after which the M-R node again functions normally.

Note: Eclipsidol is a new and extremely rare tool in the Directive's arsenal. Few Directive agents know it exists, fewer still have access to it, and it has been used in the field less than 10 times. Project Utopia does not know of the existence of eclipsidol, and the Directive hopes to maintain that advantage for as long as possible by using it only in the direst of circumstances.

Eu-Freeze

The Directive does not issue eufiber to its agents, nor does it condone its use. The substance is considered dangerous and unreliable. However, novas seem to love it, and Directive R&D has found a way to use it against them. Loaded into compact, powerful spray cans, a single dose of eu-freeze releases a cloud of gas that engulfs one normal-sized person. The gas smells awful but has no other ill-effects except against eufiber. Any eufiber contaminated with the substance "freezes" in its current state. It no longer interacts with the nova wearing it. The nova cannot use quantum points stored within the fiber or charge it with new points. Likewise, the fiber no longer attunes itself to the nova's powers or offers any armor bonus. The effects of eu-freeze last for just under 24 hours, although a good dry cleaner can get it right out. It is not water soluble.

Range: 10 feet

Area of effect: 6 feet (one human-sized person)

System: The user attacks as normal, using Dexterity + Firearms to aim the spray. Each success covers 50% of the target's eufiber clothing, reducing its effectiveness by one-half (round down). Thus, two successes cover the entire target and neutralize all exposed eufiber. Partially "frozen" eufiber has its quantum capacity lowered by one-half, rounded down.

Hypnotic Lenses

Often, operatives do not have the time or facilities to carry out an effective interrogation. The hypnotic lenses consist of a bulky headset that resembles a pair of night vision goggles. This is not a subtle device, but it is portable. When fitted, the device pries open the wearer's eyes and forces him to view a series of hypnotic images peppered with sophisticated subliminal messages, effectively hypnotizing most individuals.

System: The lenses work just like the quantum power Hypnosis, although at a relatively low level. The lenses have 5 dice to overcome the victim's Willpower. For each half-hour the victim wears the lenses, the user can roll again, up to a maximum of four times in one day. Success allows the user to plant suggestions just as with the Hypnosis power.

Klot

One of the few legal products manufactured by Kuro-Tek, Klot is a chemically and quantum-inert nova immobilizer. Klot comes as two component chemicals; when the two are mixed, they quickly become an extremely dense, sticky gray gel. Klot immediately immobilizes all but the strongest novas — it's as though they were trying to swim through tar. The difficulty to move through Klot is 13 - (dots of Mega-Strength).

Klot is most commonly used in "Klot tanks" within Directive holding facilities to prevent novas with Mega-Strength from smashing their way to freedom.

Klot does not burn, liquefy or conduct electricity, and, most importantly, it is also quantum-resistant (much in the same way that rubber is electricity-resistant). All rolls to affect Klot directly with quantum powers are at +3 difficulty.

Utopia advocates the use of Klot in situations where novas need to be safely immobilized and condones its sale to military and law-enforcement organizations, but Kuro-Tek will sell Klot to anyone willing to part with enough yen.

Once the crisis situation is resolved, Klot can be dissolved into a non-toxic slurry with an enzymatic solvent called De-Klot.

The Directive maintains five so-called "Klot tanks" in its Forgotten City facility. These are rooms of reinforced steel inside concrete bunkers which agents can fill with Klot in the space of seconds should the nova being held there become uncooperative.

Laser Microphone

The most advanced version of a technology that's been around for almost two decades, the laser microphone uses a low power beam to listen through windows and thin walls by detecting sound vibrations made by people talking on the other side. This incarnation is quite portable: The laser is the size of a pen and has a range of 3,000 meters. It has a built-in recording device and a earpiece attachment so the user can listen in while she records. Naturally, the laser must have line of sight to the target. This device only works when used on a window or thin wall of the room the user wishes to listen in on.

Lock Gun

A favored tool of law enforcement and criminals alike for many years, the lock gun quickly and easily opens any standard key lock. Simply insert the rod and pull the trigger, and the lock gun forces the lock open with ease. Of course this leaves obvious signs of tampering, but sometimes that's not an issue. Directive-issued lock guns also incorporate a built-in electronic-lock decoder. This can broadcast appropriate signals, register with card swipes and open any standard, commercial electronic lock with ease. More advanced electronic locks, such as those in Directive installations, Project Utopia headquarters and government facilities do not succumb to the standard lock gun.

Mental Noise Generator

One of the newest inventions to come out of the Directive's R&D department, the mental noise generator is a small box about the size of a cell phone. In fact, they are often incorporated into Directive issued cellular phones. Designed to foil telepathic and mental assaults on agents, the MNG sends out waves of energy attuned to the same frequencies found most commonly in telepathic communication. These disrupt attempts to use psychic abilities anywhere within 25 feet of the generator. On the down side, any nova possessing such abilities immediately senses any MNG operating in their vicinity. Thus, agents are encouraged not to use the device indiscriminately.

System: The device acts like a low level Psychic Shield, providing anyone within 25 feet two extra dots when resisting mental attacks. However, its effects are not cumulative with the quantum power Psychic Shield.

Next-Gen Listening Devices

Hidden recording devices, or "bugs," are one of the stock items for any intelligence agency. The problem with most bugs is that they can be detected, either by the signal they transmit or the electrical energy they give off while in operation. The Directive has managed to create a series of bugs that are almost undetectable. The recording mechanism is entirely mechanical, in effect a microscopic version of the original phonographs. Thus, while recording, the device emits no electromagnetic radiation and cannot be detected.

Of course, it just records in this manner. The agents who placed the bug can listen to the recordings in one of two ways: They can recover the bug and play it back, or they can activate a built in transmitter via a coded radio signal. This latter option activates an electronic function within the bug that starts transmitting (making the device detectable by normal means). These transmissions can either relay previous recordings in a short, coded burst or continue transmitting live audio to the receiver. The bug itself is just about the size of a thumbtack and can be hidden within walls, phones, electrical outlets or almost anywhere and still pick up all sounds within 50 feet.

Undercover agents often have such items disguised as buttons or simply sewn into the lining of their clothing. The bugs can then record everything the operative hears and says but remain undetectable by anyone searching them for a wire.

Night-Vision Glasses

The latest development in low-light accessories, the night-vision glasses do not work under the same principals as traditional night-vision technology. Instead, they amplify ambient light using specially designed lenses and a computer enhanced photo-real display. To outside viewers, they look like normal glasses (which tint to become sunglasses when it gets bright). From the wearer's point of view, they make the whole world crisper and clearer and allow her to see perfectly in any light. Only total darkness inhibits her vision. Most recent models also have a built-in record feature that keeps a record of everything the wearer sees for up to four hours.

Nova Restraints

Locking up a nova is seldom an easy task, yet occasionally, Directive operatives need to do just that. If Klot is not an option, nova restraints are a Directive agent's next-best friend. Nova restraints look like the normal, titanium wrist- and ankle-shackles used by law-enforcement agencies around the world. In fact, they can and do operate just like normal restraints, but they have several special features that can be activated by the owner. First, there are powerful batteries built into the thick cuffs that can deliver a powerful shock via remote control. Secondly, there are recessed needles within the cuffs, also under remote control, that can inject a powerful sedative or other drug. Finally, opening the locks requires using both a physical key and an electronic code broadcast from the controller. The controller itself is coded to the owner's fingerprints and has a voice recognition feature built into it. All together, these shackles can hold most, but certainly not all, novas.

System: The controller has a range of three kilometers. The user can use any of the following features — Shock: The restraints can deliver up to five shocks before recharging, each of which causes 6 levels of bashing damage automatically (although the target may still soak). Injection: The restraints have one built in drug dose which automatically works unless the target has a natural armor rating of 4 or more against lethal damage. The effects depend on the drug injected, usually a powerful sedative. The nova must have Mega-Stamina of 3 or more to remain conscious. Breaking the shackles requires a Mega-Strength rating of at least 2.

One-Time Code Disks

The only surefire code in existence is the one-time pad. The sender and receiver each have a set of codes that they use only once. Unless you have one of the randomly generated code pads, it's impossible to find patterns or underlying equations and, thus, break the code. The modern version of this spycraft classic uses one-time decoding disks. Operatives use their disk to encrypt an e-mail or recorded message and send it to someone with the matching disk. That person then uses his disk to decode the message. After one use, the disks are worthless. Agents in the field, especially in hostile territory or under deep cover, use these disks when reporting back to their superiors. Unless someone steals the disks (which can be keyed to an individual's fingerprints and voice), there is no way to break the code.

Portable Lie Detector

Based on traditional lie-detector technology, with a few enhancements, the portable version is a small tube that slips over the target's finger like an oversized ring. It then squeezes tight, much like having one's blood-pressure taken. The device monitors heart rate and other physical factors to determine whether or not the person is lying. Only yes and no questions work with the device.

A red light on the tube glows when it detects a lie.

System: Characters wearing the lie detector can try to fool it. This takes three successes on a Manipulation + Subterfuge role. Otherwise, it pretty accurately determines whether a person is lying or telling the truth.

The Van

A mobile intelligence command center, the Van is one of the Directive's most prized and sophisticated (and expensive) pieces of equipment. It is a large cargo van that, from the outside, looks unremarkable. Inside, it seats a driver and three passengers at computer work stations, along with bench seats in the back for four more (although with that many people, it does get crowded). Designed to allow a cell to run an entire operation from its interior, the Van has everything a team could want: encrypted cellular and radio communication; powerful computers linked into the Directive's databases and satellite information network; video and audio monitors capable of tracking up to 100 discreet bugs and hidden cameras; a built in CompReader system; a powerful engine; bulletproof windows; and armored walls and ceiling.

Stats

Safe Speed: 125

Max Speed: 200

Maneuver: 5

Passengers: 9

Armor: 3 [8]

Cost: ●●●●

Video Surveillance Gear

Miniaturization technology has made powerful, crystal-clear digital cameras a reality for everyone, and the Directive has access to the best in existence. The standard Directive spy camera is the just a one centimeter cube and can store up to 12 hours of data or transmit up to 13 kilometers. Most capture audio content as well. They can also be sent into a timed shutdown mode during which time they are virtually undetectable by most scanning devices (since they give off no electronic signature). Placing them within or adjacent to existing electronic devices makes them all the harder to detect.

V-R Lenses (or Beer Goggles)

Not all novas use blatant psychic powers to manipulate humans. Some seem to possess extraordinarily powerful personalities or amazingly attractive visages that can seriously compromise a person's better judgment. The Directive labs have produced virtual-reality lenses for glasses, which include built in earpieces, that help defend against such manipulation. They actually make the world look less real and more like a computer game. Figures remain identifiable but take on a slightly blocky, unnatural look. Sounds become more monotone, less natural. Meanwhile, grammar computers within the glasses analyze speech content and summarize it on the lens, helping the wearer cut through double-talk. Op-

eratives in the field have taken to calling these lenses "beer goggles." While these effects can be a little disorienting at first, they provide effective protection against charismatic novas.

System: The lenses effectively block out three levels of Mega-Manipulation, Mega-Charisma and Mega-Appearance. Thus, a nova with a Mega-Manipulation of 4 would have an effective Mega-Manipulation of 1 against someone wearing the lenses. The penalties for such advantages are not insignificant. The wearer's Perception is reduced by 1, and if he has Mega-Perception, it is also reduced by 1. Ranged attacks and anything else requiring accurate depth perception suffer a 2 dice penalty.

Weapons

Shock Net

The shock net is a variation on the non-lethal net gun used by a number of local law-enforcement agencies (as seen in **Aberrant: Year One**). Like its predecessor, the shock net fires a synthetic eufiber derivative net for the purpose of immobilizing a target. The shock net, however, takes it a step further by conducting an electrical charge down metallic wiring laced through the net.

System: Like the common net gun, the attacker rolls Dexterity + Firearms when firing a shock net to hit his target. Then the attacker initiates a resisted roll, his D Dexterity + Firearms vs. the target's Dexterity to determine how many dots of Dexterity the defender loses. If reduced to zero Dexterity, the target can't move. However, the net has an effective "Strength" of 5 and six "health levels" and so may be torn. Realizing the danger of this, Directive R&D installed the shock feature based on previous nova restraints. With the click of a switch, the weapon's operator may deliver an electric shock to anyone in contact with the net, doing up to10 bashing levels of damage automatic (a control on the weapon controls the amperage, so the damage may be adjusted depending on the target). Battery life allows for five such jolts.

The Banshee

A recent development of Directive R&D, the Banshee is portable sonic weapon vaguely the size and shape of a rifle. While still experimental, the Banshee has proven itself an effective non-lethal weapon against novas. The only drawback thus far is the gun's extreme fragility, which makes it inappropriate for many operations.

System: The Banshee has three different settings. The first is Shriek: At this setting the gun releases an ongoing wail above the range of human hearing. This does nothing to baselines, but any novas with Mega-Perception (and many animals) are deafened by the sound at a radius of 50 feet (150 for novas with the Hyperenhanced Hearing enhancement active). Such a nova needs to make a Resistance roll or all he is capable of doing is holding his ears and cringing. Even if the nova succeeds on this roll, all activities are at +3 difficulty while the Banshee is operating. This setting is likely to shatter nearby glass and crystal. The second setting is Thump: When fired, the Banshee emits a powerful burst of low-frequency sound designed to stun opponents. This works as a level five Stun Attack if the operator succeeds in a Dexterity + Firearms roll. The highest setting is Keen: At this level, the Banshee works much like a medical lithotriptor. However, instead of crushing kidney stones, the Banshee shatters bone, causing 6 levels of lethal damage to the target if the operator succeeds on a Dexterity + Firearms roll. Because of the internal nature of the damage, Armor does nothing to stop it.

(**Note:** As mentioned above, the Banshee is extremely fragile. Any sort of jostling, especially in a combat situation can cause the weapon to fail. After the Banshee receives a serious bump, the weapon's operator should make an Intelligence + Science roll to recalibrate the device. Failure causes the gun to shut down until it can be disassembled and repaired. A botch causes the weapon to shake itself to pieces, causing 4 levels of bashing damage to its operator.)

Ranged Weapons Chart

Type	Acc	Dmg	Range	Mnv	RoF	Clip	Conc	Mass	Cost
Shock Net	0	S	5	n/a	1	1	N	3	●●●●
Banshee	0	S	20	n/a	1	5	N	4	●●●●●

Acc: Accuracy indicates the number of dice added to the operator's dice pool.

Dmg: Indicates the damage dice pool for the weapon. S: special, see weapon's description for details.

Range: Practical range of the weapon in meters.

Mnv: Maneuvers lists special attacks available.

RoF: Rate of fire, the number of shots that can be made in a turn.

Clip: The number of times a weapon may be used before reloading.

Conc: Concealability of the weapon. N: May not be concealed at all.

Mass: The weapons weight in kilograms.

Cost: Represents the Resources needed to purchase the weapon.

Part Three: New Dramatic Systems

Running a story centered around Directive characters can take your **Aberrant** game in whole new directions. Directive based games tend to be less about the clash of super-powered novas and more about behind the scenes manipulation, intrigue and intelligence gathering. A team of Directive characters can spend an entire evening just enjoying overcoming the various obstacles associated with spying on a nova and finding out everything there is to know about him, without the subject ever becoming aware of their presence. This section focuses on new rules and dramatic systems helpful for playing such games but that are also useful in any game, especially if the Directive is the main antagonist.

Creating Directive Characters

Players might wish to create characters expressly to work in the Directive. In fact, if the players wish to have a game centered around the organization, they just about have to make characters this way. The Directive is very choosy about whom it allows into its ranks, and most novas wouldn't make the cut. There are two types of characters available to Directive players: novas and baselines.

Nova characters are created as normal with just a few restrictions. First of all, the nova cannot have any Taint at all. Not even a little bit. Secondly, the character cannot have any obvious or extremely blatant quantum powers. The Directive does not trust novas possessing such abilities and does not want the publicity such powers naturally bring.

Baseline characters are created like normal characters except you stop generation at the end of Phase One. The characters get no nova points at all. This means, obviously, that Directive baselines won't be as powerful as their nova counterparts. Well, that's the reality of the situation. Part of the fun of playing a baseline Directive member is using your normal abilities to go up against super-powered antagonists. Fortunately, Directive operatives do

The Directive is not fond of utilizing nova operatives. The following list delineates the powers Directive novas may possess. Under unusual situations (i.e., the character was a Directive agent before her eruption), the Directive *may* allow operatives with non-standard abilities to serve as operatives, but these cases are few and far between and subject to a combination of agent's discretion and the Directive's current needs.

Any combination of Mega-Attributes (so long as the agent remains discreet with their use)

Level One Powers:

Hypnosis

Intuition

Luck

Psychic Shield

Sensory Shield

Silence (see **Aberrant: Project Utopia** p. 141)

Level Two Powers:

Absorption

Armor (so long as it in no way renders the agent less human in appearance)

Boost

Disimmunize (see **Aberrant: Teragen** p. 127)

Disorient

Disrupt

Domination

Empathic Manipulation

ESP

Invisibility

Mental Blast

Premonition

Telepathy

Level Three Powers:

Cyberkinesis

Healing

Pretercognition

Furthermore, since novas do not have the full trust of the Directive, no matter what their powers, nova operatives suffer the following limits on Backgrounds:

Maximum Equipment ● ● ● ●

Maximum Rank ● ● ●

have a few advantages most baselines don't, mainly in the three special backgrounds and the technology discussed earlier in this chapter. While they might not even the playing field, they do help a little.

Final Touches

All Directive operatives have a few things in common thanks to their training. In addition to all the normal Abilities and Backgrounds purchased during character creation, Directive characters receive the following statistics automatically:

Cipher ● ● ● (The Directive protects all its members from outside scrutiny)

Resources ● ● (The Directive pays well and provides for its operatives as a safeguard against bribery)

Characters who want higher levels than those presented must spend the full point cost. For example, having a Resources of 3 would still cost 3 Background points during character generation.

Forming a Cell

The best way to run a Directive series is to organize all of the characters into a single cell (probably of the operational variety). This allows them to work together with relative independence and lets the Storyteller give them new assignments as the story needs. Cells operate out on their own and know little or nothing about the secret goings on elsewhere in the Directive. Thus, the players could portray characters who join the Directive for idealistic reasons but come to suspect it is rotten within. Alternatively, they can follow the party line and focus all their attentions on containing the nova threat. Either way (or some combination) can be lots of fun.

The Directive provides for its cells, but obviously, characters with higher Equipment and Favors backgrounds can better outfit their group. The Storyteller can even allow the players to pool their Equipment dots to get really big or rare items for the group (perhaps they're based off a submarine or have their own spy satellite). The character with the highest Rank background is obviously in charge, although players are encouraged to agree on a leader before they generate characters. Remember that novas can't lead cells, so the leadership position can compensate a player who isn't playing a quantum-imbued character.

Privacy Laws, Quantum Powers and the Intelligence Business

Prior to the first appearance of novas in 1998, most of the world's nations were already reexamining their privacy laws in the face of the increasingly pervasive Internet and other technological innovations in the information field. The sudden, incontrovertible appearance of humans with abilities such as ESP, Telepathy, Empathic Manipulation and others brought with them a whole new morass of legal problems. Laws about privacy have been redefined and expanded around the planet to encompass quantum powers. Although regulations vary from country to country, almost every nation has developed a core set of statutes.

Without exception, it is the telepathic novas that arouse the most fear when it comes to privacy issues. Our minds have always been (or at least seemed) inviolate places where no one could penetrate. Now that's no longer the case. At the same time, Telepathy and similar quantum abilities give the legal system something its never had before: a theoretically sure-fire way of telling whether or not people are lying. Human rights advocates, legal scholars, philosophers and lawmakers have been weighing benefits and rights ever since.

In all the Directive member nations (and much of the rest of the industrialized world), Telepathy is widely acknowledged as legal and reliable testimony in a court of law when performed by a court-appointed telepath. However, it has been ruled that no court or government has the right to force telepathic scrutiny upon its citizens. Telepathic probing inherently violates their right to privacy and their guarantees against self-incrimination. By extension, it is totally illegal for novas to use such powers against an unwilling target. Of course, some nations do not have such restrictions on novas, particularly under harsh and repressive regimes where telepathic screening of suspected criminals have become, if not *de rigueur*, then at least not uncommon (depending, of course, on the availability of telepaths).

The law has cracked down on other sorts of mental manipulation and probing as well. Empathic control, thought control and other psychic assaults carry penalties on par with rape or attempted murder in most civilized nations. A side effect of the wave of legal restrictions on quantum invasions of privacy has been the resulting strengthening of privacy laws in general. Countries that once had nebulous or non-existent privacy laws have passed sweeping legislation banning any kind of prying into an individual's private life and assigning harsh penalties to those who violate these laws. The United States and much of Western Europe have led the way in this legal trend.

This worldwide reaction to privacy invasions has made life a little harder for intelligence-gathering organizations like the Directive. Numerous companies now sell high-quality devices designed to scramble e-mail, detect listening devices, foil wire taps and otherwise interfere with the tools of the trade. Naturally, the Directive (and other agencies) always manage to stay one or two steps ahead of the commercial equipment, but it costs money and time. Of greater concern are the drastic penalties most countries now enforce on anyone caught violating privacy laws. While the Directive protects its own within member nations' territory, operatives working in other countries risk grave consequences — in some cases death.

One advantage the Directive enjoys over traditional intelligence groups is that it does not usually target governments. Most novas, particularly Teragen and other dangerous types, have no affiliation with any government at all. As a result, invading their privacy is not treasonous or an act of aggression against a sovereign nation. It might be illegal, but if the agents get caught, they probably won't start a war. It also means that most novas (outside of Utopia's trusted members) only have commercially available protection for their computers, phones and homes, all easily circumvented by any Directive operative with the right training.

Extreme Methods: Torture and Telepathy

Novas don't abide by the Geneva Convention or international law. Torture and uninvited telepathic probes are risks Directive operatives face every day when dealing with their quantum powered foes. Sometimes, in the course of doing their duty, the Directive itself breaks these laws as well. Its members feel that, when dealing with novas, they cannot tie one hand behind their backs just because the law says so. Although the Directive's charter prohibits such behavior, the reality in the field tends to be much different. Thus this section, which details some basic rules for resisting torture and telepathic probes.

Torture

Torture can be the old-fashioned physical kind: pain inflicted with sharp instruments and hot pokers. It can also be more psychological or subtle in nature, including drugs, sleep deprivation, ceaseless loud noises, even the classic Chinese water torture and its many variants. No matter what form it takes, torture has one simple goal: to break the victim's will to resist. It is a truism within the intelligence community that everyone breaks eventually. Once you find a lever (and pain almost always works), humans and novas alike can only put up with it for so long before they break. There is one exception to this rule: Novas with Mega-Stamina can withstand physical torment for weeks and barely notice the annoyance; for them, the torture has to be mental. Torturers are forced to get creative to extract information from these hardy souls.

In game terms, that means using up the victim's entire available Willpower pool. More extreme methods (i.e. physical torture) usually wear a target down more quickly than other methods, but eventually, the result is always the same. The Storyteller needs to determine how effective the torture is and set a duration each session must go before the victim needs to make a Willpower roll to resist. For horrifying physical assaults, it might be as often as once every five minutes. For less damaging mental tortures, it might be once every day. Of course, if the victim's a nova, the torturers need to be able to hurt him in some way in order to torture him physically.

At the end of each torture session, victims must make a Willpower roll. If they succeed, they hang in there. If they fail, they lose a point of Willpower. If they botch, they lose it all. Of course, characters may spend Willpower points for automatic successes in this effort, but obviously, that only works for a certain amount of time. If the torturers are patient and persistent, they will win in the end. The victim's only hope is to last long enough for someone to rescue him or die during the torture before he breaks (a very real possibility with more physical tortures).

Telepathy

Without training, it is hard to resist telepathic probing. A character can always foil a telepath by spending Willpower. However, if the telepath has the time and energy to keep after the target, eventually she'll get through. There are, however, several other methods a target can try in order to shake off a telepathic probe. Directive agents train long and hard to resist such mental invasions. Any operative with the Thought Discipline skill has built-in mental barriers to telepathic intrusions. Telepaths trying to break through the discipline must subtract one success for every dot of Thought Discipline the target possesses.

Those without the advantage of such training can attempt to duplicate it by filling their head with "noise" — random thoughts such as nursery rhymes, multiplication tables and so forth. Although much less effective than Thought Discipline, it can stymie a telepath for a short period of time. The character makes a straight-up Wits roll. Each success reduces the telepath's successes by one. However, the character cannot take any other action during this time, though he may be able to move, at the Storyteller's discretion. It requires all of one's concentration to effectively fill the mind with white noise. Moreover, once the telepath breaks through, the target cannot use this technique to resist any more for the remainder of the scene. Having penetrated the barrier once, the telepath's intrusion becomes too established to resist.

Blocks

The Directive also employs trained hypnotists to block out certain information within their members' minds. These blocks prevent the agent from recalling certain sensitive information unless they hear a specific code word or are in a specific location (such as their headquarters or a secure room). The Directive uses these blocks on high-ranking members to protect them against telepathic scans while out on the street. It takes a full day, sometimes more, to set up these blocks, and the process is not available to every operative (since the number of qualified hypnotists is small).

While highly effective against most telepaths, these blocks are not foolproof. A determined telepath can break through. It requires three successes in a normal probe for the telepath to even realize that the blocks exist. Breaking through a block requires a second probe and five successes. A character might well have several different blocks within his mind that the telepath must overcome individually.

Listening In: Using Bugs, Taps and Traces

The key to any successful intelligence operation is, well, intelligence. Most of a Directive operative's job takes place without the target novas ever learning they're being investigated. Like any good agency, the Directive has mastered the art of spying from afar and behind the scenes. Every intelligence and operational cell has some basic spying methods available to them around the clock. Here are the systems for using those methods in your **Aberrant** game.

Bugs and Hidden Cameras

Small, hidden listening devices and spy cameras are invaluable to the intelligence operative, and the Directive has some of the best in the business (see the technology section above). Bugs can be placed just about anywhere and usually have a listening range comparable to or slightly better than the human ear. Since most bugs are electronic devices, they emit a small amount of electromagnetic radiation. If they are using a wireless transmitter to send information back to their owner, then that is detectable as well. Bug detectors search for such emissions and sometimes include metal detectors as well. Careful operatives know where to place bugs so that they are less easily detected.

Systems: Placing a bug requires a straightforward Intelligence + Tradecraft roll. Each success means the character placed the bug that much better, making it that much harder to find.

Finding a bug requires a Perception + Investigation roll and a conscious decision to look in the right place (or search an entire room very carefully). Even then, the searcher must score more successes than the person who placed the bug. Novas with Mega-Perception get one automatic success for each dot they have. If the searcher has a quality bug detector and the bug he's searching for is emitting signals or electromagnetic radiation (note that most of the time Directive bugs do neither), then he gets 4 extra dice for his dice pool while searching.

Wiretaps

One of the big disadvantages, as far as privacy is concerned, with the modern telecommunications network is that it's remarkably easy to listen in on. In order for the Directive to monitor any conversation using commercially available phone lines or cell-phone networks, they need only punch in the request to their computers (when working in one of their member nations at least). The Directive has firmly and secretly established itself in every communications network in the United States, the Russian Confederation, Japan, the UK and Germany, as well as most of the rest of Europe. Although, theoretically, they need warrants, in practice, the Directive listens in on whom they want, whenever they want, without any problems at all.

In other countries, especially China and the lands of South America and Africa where the Directive has little presence, it takes a bit more doing. In countries with advanced communications systems, tapping into someone's phone or cell phone requires the right equipment (which fits in a standard issue briefcase) and a normal Intelligence + Tradecraft roll. In less advanced countries, it might require actual line tapping (as opposed to

computer hacking) and, thus, requires more time and two successes on that Intelligence + Tradecraft roll.

Many services advertise commercially available "secure" lines of communication. In fact, they use relatively simple encryption programs that Directive computers can cut through without missing a beat. More advanced military and corporate systems do use advanced and expensive cryptography. Given enough time, Directive computers can always break through these codes, but it might take days. An operative trying to break the code herself must have a Tradecraft of at least 3, the right programs and make three or more successes on an Intelligence + Computer Roll.

The only truly secure method of communication is to have dedicated land lines that do not link to any outside networks. The Directive uses such lines within its own facilities and even to connect different facilities within the same country. Someone who knows where to look for the line can physically tap it. Since the dedicated lines are set up to give warning when tampered with, it requires 4 success on a Intelligence + Tradecraft roll to tap the line and not be noticed. Even then, the signals traveling along the line are almost always encrypted.

Spy Satellites

There are literally thousands of satellites in orbit, looking down on the Earth in order to aid communication, watch weather trends and, of course, spy on people. Modern satellites have quite sophisticated imaging systems on them, capable of high resolution pictures down to five centimeters. On a cloudless day, these satellites can easily follow a person walking along a street miles below. When it clouds over, they can still use their infrared imaging to keep track of events below, although with less accuracy. Satellites also tie into locator beacons that emit signals or respond to transmissions from the satellite. The information from these beacons, combined with databases containing street maps and floor plans of every building in a given city, allow the satellite to track the beacon wherever it (and the person carrying it) goes.

Directive locator beacons have become quite small and can assume a variety of sizes. They fit easily onto the circuit board of any piece of electronic equipment. New versions replace the metallic anti-counterfeiting strip inside most world currency. Such strips can also be sewn into clothing or even ingested and still work. Every license plate manufactured in the Directive member nations in the past three years has such a strip implanted in it, coded to the license plate number and the car's owner. A person unknowingly carrying one or more beacons cannot go anywhere without the satellite following from above. That is, of course, assuming the satellite's looking.

There are only so many spy satellites in space, although the Directive keeps the exact number a closely guarded secret. A special branch, Space Division, is responsible for all of the Directive's orbiting watchdogs. The division itself is divided into at least 10 different cells, each responsible for a different number of satellites, so even most members of the division have no idea how many birds there really are. The Directive has two types of platforms in orbit: rotators, which move around the planet in a regular orbit, and sitters, which stay in geo-synchronous orbit above particular cities.

Any intelligence or operational cell can request the use of a spy satellite for its current operation, but that does not mean the cell will get one. The spy birds are in constant demand. Characters can use their Favors background to gain access to a satellite for short periods of time, ranging from a few hours to, at most, a few days. If, however, the administration (and the Storyteller) feel that the cell's current operation is terribly important and absolutely requires access to a satellite, it can ensure the characters have the bird for as long as they need it.

Background Checks

For the past half century, most people on Earth have left longer and longer paper trails. In the modern day, where credit and debit cards are the norm, security cameras are everywhere and much of the industrialized world does its shopping online, we leave so many traces of ourselves in the system, its hard to know where to begin. Moreover, most of this information is stored in barely protected corporate computers or government files that the Directive has unlimited access to. Thus, running a detailed background check on someone is just routine for the Directive.

When researching anyone born or living in one of its member nations or anywhere in Europe, North America, South Korea, Singapore, Taiwan, South Africa, Australia or New Zealand, the Directive can get a full credit history, legal history and the details of every bit of electronic commerce and credit or debit card use in the past decade. Moreover, it takes only a few minutes to assemble this data from the Directive's extensive data bases. Tax returns, pay checks, credit card transactions, pictures from ATM security cameras and more are collected every minute of every day, particularly if the target is a known nova. Getting the data from other countries takes more doing, including an Intelligence + Tradecraft roll.

For game purposes, access to this data is nearly instantaneous, unless the target has the Cipher background. Even then, the target's Cipher rating is reduced by one when the Directive attempts to follow her trail. Of course, the Directive knows everything about its own members, so Directive Cipher dots do nothing to inhibit its search. Simple programs can alert an operative immediately whenever a person uses her credit cards, ID card, parking pass or leaves any other electronic trace. The program immediately pinpoints the person's location, what she's buying and, possibly, a picture from any local traffic or networked security cameras along with a map highlighting the quickest way for the agents to get there.

CHAPTER FIVE: PERSONNEL MANAGEMENT

"Why the Directive?"

The Advantages of the Directive

Okay, so the Directive is this bunch of guys... who... sneak around and keep tabs on novas and Project Utopia.... And they're all kinda like the CIA or the OSS... and most of them aren't even novas themselves... and most of those who are have only Mega-Attributes or just a bunch of regular dots....

Impressed yet?

If you've turned straight from the cover of this book to this chapter, you may well think that rambling mess is what the Directive is all about. If you've read nothing more about the Directive than the material in the **Aberrant** core book, you might be under a similar misconception. In a world of erupting novas who can conceive abstract number theory in their sleep, batter down stories-high, monsoon-driven waves or upset the political balance of a nation with a well-timed wink, the Directive might even seem pretty bland. After all, it's outmanned, understaffed and untrusted, right?

Wrong. So wrong.

Why would you want to play an agent of the Directive? Because the Directive fills a vital niche in the political and social dynamic of the **Aberrant** setting. Directive agents face numerous obstacles in the course of their work, but they also receive certain concomitant benefits to which only they are privy. Project Utopia has spent many years winning the hearts and public-approval ratings of the world at large, but it has painted itself into a corner. That organization has put forward a benign, politically correct, telegenic face, thus creating a certain image that it must uphold no matter what. When the time comes for the ignoble, dirty actions necessary in pursuit of a perfect world, Project Utopia must either forego them altogether, have someone else do the dirty work or rely on the subtle ministrations of the shadowy Project Proteus. To act otherwise would mean death in the court of public opinion.

The Teragen is no better off. Consider this metaphor: Do you remember the first time you stood up to your parents with the firm, unshakeable resolve of a real adult? It was likely exhilarating — a glorious revel of self-derived authority. In that one instant, you knew that no one could deny you anything. You were finally in charge of your destiny. Such is the standard of the Teragen. These novas have realized that mere baselines are in no position to judge or control them. Novas of the Teragen are the self-declared masters of their fate.

But think back. What happened when you delivered that first, uncompromising "No" to your parents? It's at that moment in a child's life when the parents begin to drift away. They recognize that their child no longer seems to need them; thus, they withdraw the kind of support to which the child has grown accustomed. In the worst cases, some parents even see such an action as an outright rebellion. Those parents react according to years of training, punishing the child and trying to hold him back from his "freedom" to live his own life. Few parents expect their children to assert their freedom, and achieving a proper balance in such a volatile time of transition is all but impossible.

Such is also the standard of the Teragen. Separated from the masses of humanity from which they sprang, Terats have no one to rely on or trust apart from each other.

As for the Aberrants, they are truly outgunned and outmanned. Worse, they are an unorganized and disparate band of novas who have come together only out of a common fear. They huddle together for warmth around the fire of their outrage, unsure of what to do next or even who their real enemy is.

True, it is sometimes fun to play the underdog who must strive to overcome all obstacles, regardless of cost, but it's also draining. There is only so long you can go on sleeping with one eye open, eating what you can on the run and wondering if the next person you make eye-contact with is going to put a sawed-off shotgun under your chin and pull the trigger.

The Directive, however, offers many of the benefits of playing a character tied to one of the other groups, while making up for many of the deficits thereof. First and foremost, the Directive is a globe-spanning operation, answering to the most powerful countries in the world. While Utopia has broad market appeal (and children all over the world write "The Team Tomorrow Member I Admire Most Is..." essays every year in school), there are some times when too much public appeal can be detrimental. After all, which figure is more inspiring and impressive: Lee Iococa or Clive Cussler's Dirk Pitt? Power and public appeal don't always make for the most exciting lives. By the same token, playing a Project Proteus operative may offer a Utopian series the option of cloak and dagger intrigue, but Proteus operatives are constrained by the veil of absolute secrecy they *must* maintain at any cost. Agents of the Directive come out ahead because, even though they operate on the sly, they are at least allowed to let slip the fact that they exist. Of course, there are times when diversionary and covert procedures are necessary, but those missions are more the exception than the rule for Directive agents.

At the same time, Directive agents are *not* as popular or well known as the ruck and run of Utopians. Certainly, the interests of the two organizations will clash at times, and in many such cases, the Directive will seem the underdog. After all, the Directive is a younger, less "noble" organization in much of the public's opinion. A Directive series offers a more appealing version of the underdog saga. Sure, the Directive has an uphill battle to fight if it's going to cross paths with Utopia, but it's not completely overmatched. After all, agents of the Directive have the resources of their home countries to draw upon. Even against stacked odds, Directive agents have a fighting chance when the needs of the few just have to outweigh the needs of the many.

But how exactly does the prospect of playing a Directive character beat the awesome thrill of playing a Teragen nova who's careless of Taint and still reveling in his own power? The answer is simple: There is no comparison. That is to say, a Directive series is so different from a Teragen series that there is no way to say one is better than the other. If you're all about creating a mutated walking god who cares for naught but himself and who has the power to back up any cavalier statement of his own worth that he cares to make, then, frankly, the Directive doesn't have much to offer you. (In fact, check out **Aberrant: Teragen**, if that's what you're interested in.)

However, if you like the thought that you have a duty to protect your nation's interests in this new golden age, you've made the right decision by coming here. If you feel confident relying on the combined military might of multiple countries and your own specialized nova allies, then sign on now. If the idea of standing up for all un-erupted mankind against the excesses of the Übermenschen appeals to you, you have chosen wisely. The Directive is looking for people who think that way, and that's what Directive series' are all about.

A Change of Pace

Let's face it — there are only so many ways to create Mega-Whatever, Quantum-Slag-Granite-Bolting bad guys to throw against your Mega-Everything-having, Forcefield-activating, Hyperrunning good guys. By the same token, there are only so many times your players'

indestructible siege-engines-on-legs can walk through ranks of armored vehicles, laughing in godlike mirth while the puny humans wail away ineffectually. That is to say, it takes work to continually challenge and surprise nova protagonists in an **Aberrant** series without just stacking the odds against the characters so heavily that they either break under the strain or get so inhumanly powerful they become unplayable. It can be done, but the constant demand for each episode in a series to be even more entertaining, exciting and dramatic than the last can be trying for even the most experienced Storytellers.

However, a Directive-based series offers a refreshing alternative to having to top yourself constantly with bigger, badder enemies. Directive stories rely heavily on stealth, cunning, image and ingenuity, as less powerful beings pit their talents against novas. You may even run stories in which no novas figure prominently, yet the Directive agents face just as much of a challenge against baseline antagonists. It is entirely possible to run an engaging, memorable Directive story in which very few novas, if any, appear to menace the characters. By keeping said novas in reserve, you highlight their power and the distance at which some of them stand removed from humanity in much sharper relief. In so doing, you make novas much more iconic and godlike than they already are, which allows you to use them to much more dramatic effect than is possible in a story where everyone and his brother seems to be funneling quantum energy like frat boys at a Saturday-night kegger. Think how different and uninspired Bram Stoker's *Dracula* would have been if Jonathan Harker, Lucy and Van Helsing had all been vampires, leading a charge of night-stalkers against the inscrutable count. Doubtless, it would have been exciting, but it would have lacked the depth and emotion that the original has. By setting mortal, comparatively frail protagonists against a single opponent who is more than capable of destroying any one of them individually, Stoker creates a feeling of growing horror and a greater sense of triumph when the outmatched humans finally prevail. With a judicious application of nova-strength adversaries, you can create just that powerful an effect in your own Directive stories.

Perspective

The most important thing a Directive game will give you as Storyteller or player is a sense of perspective. The **Aberrant** core book gives you the game from the nova perspective, and even this book focuses on how the activities of the Directive affect and are affected by novas. Frankly, that's to be expected, as this game is about the advent of these super-beings and how they change the world around them. However, what **Aberrant** is really about is responsibility. Be it the responsibility to your world to make it a better place, the responsibility to yourself to take charge of your own destiny or the responsibility to uphold some more abstract ideal to which you feel dedicated, most of the themes in the game can be traced back to that one word.

The Directive, therefore, adheres to that overriding theme as well. However, instead of saying, "You are now a nova; you have a responsibility to do _____," stories about the Directive illustrate the responsibilities of *Homo sapiens novus* from the opposite end. The **Directive** book filters the actions of novas through the lens of baseline perception, hopefully motivating your players to think about the consequences of the cavalier use of power. Some players may find it great fun to have their characters go on a rampage, Quantum Bolting any opposition into submission from high overhead, while every imaginable countermeasure bounces harmlessly off their Forcefield-reinforced Armor. If they find such destructive expressions of their "characters'" personalities a good time and a worthwhile roleplaying experience, watch what happens when you put them in the shoes of an Alpha Division blue-and-white team facing an equally unstoppable enemy. Better yet, send them off on a reconnaissance mission with a cell of characters who are not combat-trained. Let them merely contemplate the difficulties of trying to out-think a nova many times smarter than they are. Watch them squirm as they try to figure out how best to sneak past the nova with Mega-Perception. Try not to laugh as the characters try to overtake a nova with Mega-Stamina. If they're on the ball, your players will get the lesson and temper themselves

in the future. If they're really paying attention, they might even learn something.

Yeah, whatever....

Are you that kid who always got picked on by the bigger kids? Are you the one who always ended up getting sand kicked in your teeth at the beach? If so, the Directive offers you the perfect chance to vent your long frustration. Remember, as the Storyteller, you can let happen whatever you desire. Create the most foul, despicable novas you can think of. Inflate their egos higher than the loftiest heights of hubris, and set them loose on your world. Then, when things are going great for the fictional pricks, bring in your troupe of Directive characters. Have your fictional, bad-guy novas get the better of the characters a few times, throwing them off, filling the jerks with an overblown sense of their own importance. Then, let your players' team set the novas up, tear them down and leave them wondering just what the hell happened. Now, when things can't seem to get any worse for these novas, have the players reveal that their characters are nothing more than smart, canny humans with no quantum powers or Mega-Anythings. Let these constructs of yours know that the little guy finally won the day without having to act like a bully to do it.

In the end, *that's* what Directive series' are all about.

Themes and Moods

Themes

Theme is the concept that defines what a story, or part of a story, is "about." Separate from the plot and drama of the story, theme is the unifying motif or idea that captures the spirit of a story without ever being stated directly. If presented properly, the theme will show itself off, though you as the Storyteller need never tell your players what it is. If the theme is strong enough, your players will just know what it is, even if they can't quite put it into words. Most of all, a well-presented theme will make your players *think* about what they're seeing and doing. More than anything, themes serve to make the stories you tell more real and lasting than simple one-dimensional series.

The main theme of **Aberrant** is one of power and its intrinsic responsibility. Any story incorporates that theme in some way. **Aberrant: The Directive** incorporates that theme in two ways. On one hand, the Directive exists to combat excess. Be it the excesses of a nova who has just come into his powers or evidence of Project Utopia abusing its authority, the Directive enforces those entities' responsibility to use their powers appropriately. Where those excesses cross swords with the Directive's member nations' interests, the Directive takes action.

On the other hand, Directive chronicles also rely on Directive members' responsibility to their home countries. The Directive makes no secret of the fact that the organization exists to ensure the national interests of its members, and its operatives are expected to act in a manner upholding those interests. And yet, in these new, exciting times, the world is shrinking faster than ever before. The phrase "global community" is becoming less a pipe dream and more a reality, thanks to the efforts of the world's novas. Can one person really be expected to uphold the values of just one country in such a world? The theme of responsibility and loyalty should call just these questions to the fore.

Moods

Moods, unlike themes, are not so central to the meaning of a story. Moods focus on the feelings and emotions your story inspires, and they are more apt to change, whereas themes are more stable. However, like themes, moods do not need to be spelled out to be effective. In fact, if you find that you have to tell your players what mood you're trying to achieve, you aren't doing something right.

In running a series, you express mood mainly through the way you tell a story, relying almost solely on the words you use. If you are trying to evoke a feeling of gloom, you would describe the drab, washed-out colors that pervade your setting, maybe throwing in a nod to the heavy fog or the way the buildings all around seem to loom menacingly overhead. If you say nothing more than, "You get a feeling of gloom as you sneak down the alley," your players miss out on the richness of the world you're trying to create. At the same time, you convey mood through the nonverbal cues your roleplaying setting exudes. Your own mannerisms and tone of voice affect your listeners most readily. A somber, reserved tone of voice best carries the aforementioned gloominess, whereas a breathy staccato would better suit a harrowing chase or gunfight between Directive agents and a nova malcontent in an area crowded with baseline civilians. Other factors contribute to mood as well, such as how brightly your gaming space is lit, how comfortable your seating arrangements are, the weather outside and any music you might have playing as ambient background noise.

The following moods are ones that Directive stories and series are most apt to evoke:

Paranoia

Can he hear what I'm thinking? He should have been too smart to walk into this trap. What if I try to shoot him and he dodges the bullet? Or just stands there laughing? What's he going to do to me if he catches me out here recording his conversations? I saw him flip over a speeding car with his bare hands once… would I even feel it if he hit me, or would it all be over too fast?

Novas are the most terrifying foes a baseline agent will ever match skills with. Nova powers are so all-encompassing that every nova has the potential to do literally anything, and humans just can't compete. However, what makes dealing with novas in an adversarial capacity so frightening is the fact that many novas look almost entirely human. How would you know if the man in front of you could actually bend steel bars, tamper with your memory or even force you to do yourself harm? If you're using a laser microphone to eavesdrop on two Teragen malcontents, how can you really be sure that one (or both) of them can't detect the intrusion? And what if the rumors of a conspiracy within Project Utopia are true? Is there really a secret group of spies and assassins lurking in the shadows, watching you while you're watching Project Utopia?

Questions like these plague agents of the Directive, adding tension, drama and panicked conflict to Directive series.

Patriotism

As the members of the Directive join the organization in order to safeguard their national interests, and it chooses its agents very carefully, it stands to reason that agents of the Directive will feel a particular loyalty and devotion to their country. While avoiding stereotypes, you can play up the mood of patriotism by planting national symbols in your descriptions or by setting your antagonists directly against your characters' home countries. You can even create a rich dynamic within mixed groups of Directive agents by playing the interests of opposing nations against each other. Or, for a twist, set the characters stated goals against the best interest of their home countries for the greater good of the Directive or the entire world. Will the characters choose duty over patriotism? Crossing this mood with one of anxiety is an excellent way to build internal conflict in your characters' hearts, which helps to develop them into more real, complex characters.

Stereotypes

Since many Directive series ideas will incorporate action in many national theaters, you may be tempted to rely on stereotypes for ease of description and to keep the action moving briskly. After all, stereotypes exist for a reason, don't they? What could be the harm in glossing over the description of some foreign national, letting the players' minds fill in the appropriate gaps, all in the name of maintaining story rhythm?

For the most part, there is no harm in doing so. However, using stereotypes out of ignorance (i.e., because the stereotype is all you know about another culture) can seriously short-change your game. If you don't understand a national mind-set on more than a superficial level, you run the risk of creating one-dimensional, cardboard characters that add nothing to the story or its depth. After all, not every Russian is a vodka-swilling hirsute, low-kicking Cossack, nor every Japanese man a camera-toting, chain-smoking business robot. If you rely too much on stereotypes merely because they're stereotypes, your players will notice, and they'll have less respect for your descriptive abilities.

Awe

The overriding mood of **Aberrant** in general, awe, applies just as handily to a Directive series. After all, the mirror of awe is fear, and the Directive formed as much out of fear as anything. Comprising predominantly baseline agents, the roster of Directive operatives stands in awe of its quarry and the far-reaching effects novas have on the destiny of the world. How can you help but stare agape as you catch your first face-to-face glimpse of the man whose paper trail you've been chasing and that man winks a too-beautiful eye before flying away in a shower of iridescent sparkles? Nothing compares to meeting a nova in person, even one you've deemed your enemy.

At the same time, the common man stands in awe of the Directive. Sure, the Directive employs nova agents and special forces, but even the baseline staff is impressive. Combining the best elements of MI6, the CIA, the FSB, SOBRE and the SS (with a healthy supply of the most advanced blacktech on the market), the Directive cuts a remarkable figure when it goes to work. There's something to be said for a cell of well-trained men and women in suits or fatigues securing an area in professional, silent precision and flashing a badge authorized by five of the most powerful nations in the entire world. Having Quantum powers does not automatically render a nova blasé. Some novas can't help but be intimidated by such coordinated and far-reaching shows of force. The confidence and image that goes along with being a member of the Directive is one of that agent's major tools of manipulation, so play it up when your characters are on the job.

Conflicts

The driving force behind any story is conflict. While not necessarily dependent on *combat*, conflict refers to people or situations that bar your stories' characters from their goals. Both physical and psychological in nature, conflicts make your stories interesting, and striving to win out in said conflicts gives your characters something to do. Conflicts that apply to Directive-based stories include:

Baselines vs. Novas

Stories of the Directive, more so than any type of **Aberrant** series, cast novas in an antagonistic role. The Directive came into being as a means of observing what affect novas would have on the social and political dynamics of the world, and that mind-set naturally filters the world's shining demigods though a lens of suspicion. For every adoring civilian who gazes admiringly upon the glorious deeds of Team Tomorrow, a paranoid dictator hides behind a desk, calculating the damage total from the last Utopian raid against his state-funded "labor camp." For every open-minded supporter at a Teragen-rights rally, 10 National Guard troops have to sit through yet another class on containing the perpetrators of nova-terrorism. Thus, the Directive arises. When conflict does break out, the Directive stands up for the cause of humanity.

However, this conflict demonstrates itself even within the Directive itself. Although it's proportionally small, a percentage of Directive field agents are themselves novas. While not as high-profile or flashy as the novas on Team Tomorrow or in the XWF, these Directive novas fill an important role in the organization's operations. Yet, conflicts brew best between those who work together often. Suppose a Directive nova grows tired of working for "the humans" against "[his] own kind" and tries to defect. Or maybe a Teragen nova tempts him to do just that. In either case, this struggle hits close to home, where it's to be most feared.

Security vs. Freedom

The second most important conflict that can arise in a Directive story is that of security vs. freedom. The Directive's work is invaluable to the interests of its member nations — to the whole world, some would argue — but it isn't particularly nice. The Directive taps phones, monitors e-mail, employs shotgun microphones and does an awful lot of sneaking around in the course of its job, all to fulfill its perceived duty to mankind. However, there comes a point when too much surveillance becomes unbearable. At what point does monitoring your potential enemy in an attempt to arm yourself against future conflict become an intrusion on the rights of those for whom you're doing your job? Would you, as a civilian, allow some cabal of secret police to search your home from top to bottom on the off-chance that the

search might turn up some heretofore undiscovered danger to your family? Would you submit to a mandatory drug test at work designed to ferret out delinquent influences on the job, even though you knew that you were not such a one yourself? If the government deemed your cultural heritage "potentially dangerous," would you be able to stand idly by as uniformed watchdogs prowled your neighborhood looking for signs of subversion?

You must ask yourself these questions and more as you play Directive characters and run Directive stories. They make great emotional hooks that force characters to examine their motives for doing what they do.

Organizations vs. Individuals

Similar to the preceding category, the conflict between organizations and individuals is particularly evocative in Directive stories. Individually, novas have the power to change the world. Whether he did so intentionally or not, Divis Mal inspired the Teragen movement singlehandedly. Through the will to survive and see justice done, André Corbin founded the Aberrants. Vladimir Sierka saved Russia from bitter internal dissolution almost overnight. Some novas set out to change the world, others do so by default, but in every case, each one is an individual.

However, the Directive is a collection of like-minded agents who set themselves in opposition to these novas. Powerful though they may be, are even the heralds of the new age capable of standing up to such odds? While the strength of the baselines lies in numbers, how ethical is relying on the pack mentality to overcome a single powerful foe?

The Establishment vs. the Unknown

One cannot look at the Nova Age without seeing the influence of such novas as Geryon, the Newsman and Divis Mal. Novas are human beings with human motivations, and not all humans are altruistic or noble when given the power to bring their ambitions to fruition. It is unavoidable that some novas will pose a danger to those around them, despite the best wishes of those who look on. However, since an erupted Mazarin-Rashoud node grants an infinite scope of power to a new nova, there is no way to predict accurately just what sort of danger novas of various stripes will pose.

Yet, it is the Directive's job to see to the interests of its member nations and all of humankind, and troubleshooting various nova-related dangers is certainly in those interests. As the entire world becomes new again, these agents must determine what aspects present dangers to the peace and stability that has reigned for so long. What nova powers are inherently dangerous to mankind? Which novas themselves harbor the potential to abuse their powers? Which countries are taking advantage of the changes taking place, and how do those actions affect the countries around them? The agents of the Directive must answer these questions, and quickly, before the rapid tide of change that marks the new millennium washes over them and leaves them behind in a world not of their making. Otherwise, all their work will have been in vain.

Troubleshooting

In designing a Directive series, you may find yourself at a loss. Some of the most common questions surrounding the creation of such a series include: How do I keep my baseline spies alive when they're facing nova foes? How do I keep my nova agents and baseline agents equal in the players' eyes? How do I give the Directive a chance when institutions like Project Utopia have eyes everywhere?

The answer to these questions and others which might otherwise make you shy away from the Directive are simple — on paper, at least. First, you must council your players to choose their battles carefully. If you construct a nova antagonist with enough dots in Armor, Mega-Stamina and Forcefield, it won't matter how many big guns your players' characters bring to bear. If they challenge Divis Mal to chess, they're going to go down in flames as he declares checkmate after three moves. The hunt for Totentanz isn't going to be ended by five plucky adventurers in blue and white. There will arise circumstances in which the characters should not be able to prevail, and they should accept that with a minimum of agonizing.

At the same time, it is important to make sure that your players know and *use* their characters' strengths. While a cell of baseline Directive agents might not be able to take down an international nova criminal, the cell is certainly capable of laying a cunning trap from which the nova won't be able to escape. The Directive may not be as popular or broadranging as Project Utopia, but it is also much more free to act in public. Furthermore, Directive agents are privy to a wealth of classified information that's off-limits even to Utopians, and Directive agents have the backing of five of the most powerful countries in the world. Being clever and wisely using the resources at your disposal will go a long way toward keeping your Directive characters competitive with the power players of the Nova Age.

As far as keeping nova and baseline Directive characters equal goes, you have to take a fairly active role in your players' character-creation process. The Directive only hires novas with subtle powers or a high degree of the Dormancy Background. After all, it would not do to have silver-skinned juggernauts of destruction working for you as covert operatives. Restricting your players to Mega-Attribute nova characters or novas who display no overt quantum powers provides you with easily manageable nova characters with whom baseline characters can interact and even compete on a more level playing field.

The best advice against the potential problems inherent in running a Directive game, however, is to tailor your stories to your characters and give them achievable goals. Don't be afraid to challenge them, but don't stack the odds too high against them without giving them ample opportunity to win the day. If you're stuck for ideas, read on for some suggested stories to which the Directive is particularly suited.

Story Ideas
The Early Days

Hallowell stepped into the room and flipped on the fluorescent lights without a word. The two armed toughs flanking the door blinked, but the Russian seated at the desk in the center of the room didn't flinch. Hallowell dismissed the guards and planted himself opposite the spy.

"You're with MI6," the Russian said as Hallowell cleared his throat to speak. "Seventeen years of service to the crown. No reports left unfiled; no investigation abandoned in all that time. A near-perfect record of apprehending international criminals on English soil. Very impressive."

"Who the devil do you think you are?" Hallowell sputtered, caught off guard by the unflappable Russian's audacity. "You're here to answer charges of espionage against the crown, not show off information you've obviously—"

"Research," the Russian corrected. "Not espionage. Directors Ilyanovich and Lathrop assigned me to research your viability as a potential recruit. The fact that you discovered me at all closes the case, as far as I'm concerned."

Hallowell leaned across the desk aggressively, but humored the Russian all the same. "A potential recruit for what?"

The Directive did not spring fully formed from the mind of Andrei Srebrianski at the turn of the century. It's inception, formation and implementation took hard work and a great deal of research. In its original form, the Directive was to be a solely Russian enterprise with Petr Ilyanovich at its head. However, as Ilyanovich and his agents came across obstacles barring them from their goals (mostly in the form of unsympathetic foreign governments and counterintelligence measures in place since before the Cold War), Ilyanovich knew that he had to branch out in order to achieve the goals of the Directive. Acting on intelligence he and his most trusted FSB agents had been gathering since before the Moscow Crash, Petr approached representatives of the major players in the global intelligence game in hopes of inviting them to join in his venture.

The days of collecting that intelligence, making initial notes on nova threats and recruiting converts to the cause present some interesting challenges. You can take the role of agents assigned to recruit new Directive operatives — convincing them of the rightness of your cause — or newly recruited agents, helping steer the course of the Directive's future. You can also create stories that take place before the Directive had formed in its entirety, pitting your covert intelligence-gathering skills against not only your targets but suspicious non-member nations like the United States or Japan as well. If the characters of such a story are caught by future member nations, perhaps their efforts will decide whether the nation joins or not.

Paranoia and desperation mark the earliest days of

the Directive, before it became a publicly accepted organization, so be sure to play up those aspects of the story as well.

Politics, Politics, Politics

"I fear that our English allies will not appreciate being assigned to this particular duty," Toshiro Masai said to his superior. "Otherwise, the plan is without flaw."

"One thing you must learn about the English," Mitsu Nakamura said quietly, "is how to convince them that your interests are their interests. Where we see an opportunity to capture and recruit an active elite of the DeVries Agency, the English see us asking for trouble with the nation that retained the elite's services."

"An understandable concern," Masai offered helpfully.

"Only if you have not considered all the facts," Nakamura said, giving her subordinate a withering glance. "This elite is operating in Hong Kong, and it would be all to easy for the Chinese to suspect English involvement and disturb the isolationist wall the United Kingdom hopes to build, even if such suspicions are ill-founded. By removing the elite from his operation before he is noticed or missed, we actually save Great Britain more trouble in the future. And we gain a valuable asset for future missions."

"And what of the English concern?" Masai asked demurely, looking at the floor.

"If need be, I will force the issue with the Directive's other heads and make sure that the favor I end up owing Lathrop is relatively minor."

The most potentially disastrous aspect of the Directive is its capacity to fly apart into disparate, isolated broods of cagey intelligence professionals if the delicate international balance between its member nations is not maintained. Hostilities may have cooled between the nations themselves, but each government involved in the Directive remembers its history of conflict. Events like the Russo-Japanese War and the Cuban Missile Crisis (not to mention two World Wars) stand between the ideals of the Directive and isolated nationalistic dynasties of paranoid world powers. The national interests of each Directive member might not coincide with those of the others, and a careful give-and-take exists between them in order to keep them all happy.

Stories of this type can take three distinctly different flavors. In one, the characters make up a cell of multinational agents who uphold the broad goals and ideals of the Directive. They take great pains to placate the worries of each member nation, playing the entire field to see to everyone's interests and maintain peace internally. In the second type of political story, the characters make up a cell of agents from the same country. They also uphold the Directive's ideals, but they focus solely on the interests of their own country. Not only must they accomplish

their missions, they must also see that their own nation's interests prevail. Yet in order to maintain the integrity of the Directive, they must go about their nationalistic agenda subtly, so as not to seem to be opposing the efforts of other member nations directly. The third type of political Directive story involves your players' characters running damage control against an event with the potential to destroy the Directive. Be it from outside factors (like a global conspiracy) or internal matters (corrupt agents or infiltrators), the Directive stands on the brink of dissolution, and the characters must prevent that from happening while still dealing with the threat.

A Mole in the Ranks

Dear Beta Division:

Consider this report my last, and consider it the most truthful. For months, I have convinced the novas of the Teragen that I had grown disgruntled with the American government and wished to live among my own kind. I made them believe that I felt myself superior to the unenlightened masses of hairless monkeys that cling to the reins of power of this world. I made them believe that I was one of them. They offered to accept me and challenge me and help me reach my full potential.

It's time to stop deceiving myself. I have been telling them the truth all along. Consider this report my resignation from your organization and your simian dynasty.

—Jesse Hooks

The Operation Turncoat debacle taught the Directive a valuable lesson about missions of infiltration where novas are concerned. In attempting to dig up information on the novas of the Teragen, the Directive lost a valuable nova agent and gained a dangerous enemy. In the wake of that failure, new methods of infiltration capable of fooling suspicious novas must be developed, so as not to lose the opportunity to collect valuable inside information that can't be gathered any other way.

Infiltration stories are some of the most tense Directive stories that can be told. Preparing for an infiltration operation involves research, reconnaissance and possibly even kidnapping, if you're replacing a person with an imposter agent. Most infiltration operations are limited in scope, requiring a quick in-and-out pace, lest the deception be discovered as it lingers on. Long-term infiltrations run the greatest risk of discovery, so small-scale infiltrations designed around the collection of relatively few pieces of intelligence are ideal. Thus, infiltration stories make excellent interlude or one-shot stories. They also rely on the quick wits and improvisational abilities of the character(s) involved, especially when those he's spying on can potentially read his mind, hear the accelerated pace of his heart, solve Fermat's theorem for some number greater than two and squeeze coal into diamonds.

Eruption on the Job

When the quiet, authoritative voice coming from upstairs cracked, Lewis knew that his partner had found *their quarry. He chambered a round into his pistol and moved cautiously toward the run-down flat in which the aberrant was hiding. He could hear Lakewell giving orders to the nova hiding inside, then he heard a tell-tale high-pitched whine that almost certainly signified that their quarry was charging up for a lethal blast of energy. Lewis started running, yelling for Lakewell to get away, when, without warning, his body flew into a blur of motion. The door loomed large in front of him, and he was inside. One corner, two, and he was up the stairs. The aberrant stood in front of Lewis' partner, crackling with deadly energy. Lakewell was slowly raising his gun, like a corpse's limb drifting lazily under water. Lewis moved and bowled over the nova, just in time to send the deadly bolt wide of his partner's body. Lewis and the nova crashed into the wall, which knocked the unsuspecting nova unconscious. The melting sensation faded, and Lewis let out the breath he had taken outside to yell his warning. Lakewell stood frozen, goggling in shock.*

"What happened?" Lakewell said.

"I don't know," Lewis whispered, horrified. "It happened too fast."

It's bound to happen. The stress of a job that puts agents in opposition with novas, Project Utopia, rival intelligence agencies and criminal organizations is bound to trigger the eruption of an agent's M-R node. When such a thing happens, and the initial wave of confusion and excitement ends, what do you do? Do the other agents of the new nova's cell shun him, raise him up as a hero, view him with jealousy or hand him over to their superiors as a liability? Setting your characters up with an assignment then dropping this plot hammer on them is a tough test of loyalty and acceptance that will help round out the characters as they deal with this unexpected turn of events.

Alternative Story Material

Remember that the setting material presented in these books about your storytelling game is not necessarily "canon." While there are plenty of potential story hooks in each **Aberrant** supplement and a potential gold mine exists in the core rulebook itself, you are free to twist and recast any of the information through any perceptual filters you desire. Anything that allows you to tell an interesting story that your players enjoy being a part of is worth the time and effort you put into it, no matter how far afield it ends up being from what we publish.

Therefore, if you want to cast Project Utopia as the Fourth Reich with Project Proteus as its terrible *Schutzstaffel*, do it. If you find it more dramatic to portray the Teragen as an embattled minority group of superhumans (reminiscent of that comic-book group that rhymes with "heck's men"), do it. If you see the Aberrants as revolutionaries more dangerous than the IRA could ever hope to be, don't hesitate to describe them as such. If you see the Directive as nothing more than a group of jumpsuited fascist enforcers of decadent, paranoid dictators bent on world domination, show your players what Big Brother can really do. Want a real change of pace? Set your game in a world in which all novas have Mega-Attributes, rather than quantum powers, and name the Directive as the agency chartered to investigate them.

Creating alternative settings for **Aberrant** games is not easy, but it can be a lot of fun if you've somehow managed to exhaust every potential story in the "official" **Aberrant** setting. Just remember to warn your players before hand, and keep your alternate setting consistent.

References

For reference on what it might feel like to be part of the Directive, check out these movies, comics, television shows and books:

Highlander: The Series — Pay particular attention to the depiction of the Watchers.

DC Comics' *Batman* titles — See how one man can overcome outrageous odds and a motley assortment of foes, all without a lick of super power.

The short-lived *Chase* series, also from DC Comics — No better source exists to illustrate the recruitment, eruption and early cases of a Directive agent.

The original *Firearm* series by Malibu Comics — Alec Swan is the quintessential baseline Directive agent struggling to deal with a world where superpowered "ultras" are revered.

Any book, movie or story about James Bond — One dashing agent with the resources of the English crown behind him.

True Lies — The "Omega Sector" in this movie could just as easily have been a division of the Directive.

Wicked City — Japanese animation in which the main characters are part of the "Demon Squad," the sector of the government designated to deal with threats of a supernatural nature.

The X-Files — Shadowy, secretive, rationalizing weird events that defy imagination every week and devoted to the common man's struggle against the greater forces that gather around the reins of power. What more do you need?

American Gladiators — Extremely campy and long-since cancelled, this sports television show pitted nonprofessional contestants against larger-than-life "Gladiators" with names like Laser, Turbo and Blaze in creative, rigorous, pseudo-military contests of athletic skill. If you remember the trepidation on some of the contestants faces as they squared off against the Gladiators, you get a feel for what its like to match wits with a nova adversary when you have no nova powers to call upon. You may also remember the thrill when one of the "average" contestants won through against a Gladiator despite all odds. That's what the Directive's all about.

Hunter: The Reckoning — Although **Aberrant** and the Trinity Universe are settings unrelated to those of White Wolf's World of Darkness releases, the **Hunter** game offers a unique perspective on what it feels like to be a secretive society of "regular Joes" in a world populated and controlled by super-powerful beings with goals not always in mankind's best interest.

Wrap Up

In the end, remember that you're buying and playing this game material to have fun. If you feel constrained by any of it, feel free not to incorporate it into your stories. Use this book as a set of guidelines, rather than an empirical text. Don't be a slave to highfalutin' literary concerns either. Sometimes it's best to give the players what they want, even if what they want does happen to seem cliche or stereotypical to you. There's a lot of fun to be had by setting James Bond, Nick Fury, Bruce Wayne and Taki Renshoboru against the Hulk, Skeletor, Doctor Doom and Fu Manchu and seeing what comes out in the end. This game can run the gamut from action-adventure to camp to horror to pulp to suspense, so don't be afraid to experiment. There's something for everyone.

APPENDIX: FIELD PERSONNEL

Director Arnold Harris

Background: Arnold Harris is a pragmatist and a patriot. When the demands of his job in the Central Intelligence Agency conflicted with his marriage of 21 years, he moved out of his home and asked for a divorce. When Project Utopia offered him a position in its New York complex that included a high-risk investment opportunity in the Project itself, Harris politely turned the recruiter down. When the Virginia Military Institute — from which he graduated with high honors — offered him the position of president, he turned that offer down as well. Ever since his appointment to the position of Deputy Director of the CIA, nothing distracted Harris from his determination to do his job and do it well.

As was the case in the lives of so many others, however, the eruptions of the first novas changed everything for Arnold Harris. Unafraid of the changes that slowly overtook more and more citizens around the world, Harris was not overawed by the novas' unexplained appearance. Instead, he recognized the accumulation of so much power in the hands of so few for what it was: a potential threat to the sovereign power of the United States. Working with Assistant Secretary of Defense Elliot Stinson, General Thomas Eddicott and Captain Charles Moring, Harris organized the first field trials of American novas in a military capacity. Frightened by the destructive power he witnessed, Harris withdrew from the effort, but not without first recommending to then-President Schroer (and later to President Pendleton, despite her initial distaste for the idea) that the United States continue its program of recruiting and training nova elites.

After the tests, Harris used the resources at his command to maintain constant vigilance against possible threats novas might pose to the United States. He supported the goals of Project Utopia initially as well. From a utilitarian standpoint, the Project seemed to be the best mechanism in place for keeping the scions of the new age in check. However, as the Project's goals became less distinctly American in nature and grew more catholic, Harris' favor for it evaporated. While the Project continued to do good for the world at large, he could not ignore the fact that it was really becoming a power in and of itself. Harris relayed his concerns to President Schroer, and American policy toward Project Utopia remained cool until Randel Portman's election.

When members of the fledgling Directive approached Elliot Stinson, Arnold Harris saw in the organization the natural outcome of the world's most powerful nations' desire to capitalize on the nova phenomenon. The nations of the world, he knew, would need information on the ways in which the world was changing in order to maintain stability and keep pace. During Elliot Stinson's trip to Moscow, Harris met with President Schroer at Camp David and impressed upon him the necessity of devoting American support to the growing, worldwide initiative. When Stinson returned from Moscow — convinced of the same necessity — the President recommended to him that Harris be put in charge of the American contribution.

Resigning as Deputy Director of the CIA to assume his new position, Director Harris made an immediate impression on the other leaders of the Directive. He brought to the table information on novas and on Project Utopia that his CIA agents had been collecting over the preceding years. Also, despite his stated suspicion and distrust of novas, he argued for the inclusion of nova agents in the Directive's ranks. His thorough, exhaustive argument convinced even Petr Ilyanovich — who was most strongly opposed to the idea — of the merit of doing so. He pointed out that to eschew the incredible collection resource nova agents represented would be worse than foolish, especially when most of the Directive's subjects of study were novas themselves.

Now, the impression Director Harris made on his peers rests firmly in the minds of his subordinates. Those who serve under him know him to be a man of implacable practicality, regardless of his opinion on whatever issue may be at hand. They know that he could not have risen to the position he now holds without putting common sense and the nation's best interest first.

Image: Well in his late 60s, Harris remains in good shape and good health. His muscles show the signs of his age, but he remains a thick, stocky bull of a man. He often wears an expression of concentration on his deeply lined face, except in the presence of the novas under his command. When addressing those agents, his face becomes carefully blank, revealing no emotion whatsoever. Director Harris moves with stiff, brisk precision, due to his years of service in military intelligence before he joined the CIA. He wastes no energy. On or off the job, Harris dresses in unremarkable, if expensive, suits. His clothing is never

Gear: Doing most of your work behind a computer, you need little in the way of personal equipment to carry out your duties. For safety's sake, however, you carry a .45 in a shoulder holster, a canister of eu-freeze in a belt case and a pressurized dispenser of moxinoquantamine. You also wear a radio earpiece while on the job to maintain contact with agents on assignment in the field.

Nature: Leader

Allegiance: Directive

Attributes: Strength 2, Dexterity 2, Stamina 3, Perception 3, Intelligence 4, Wits 3, Appearance 2, Manipulation 3, Charisma 2

Abilities: Academics 1, Analysis 5, Awareness 3, Biz 1, Brawl 1, Bureaucracy 2, Command 4, Computer 1, Drive 2, Endurance 2, Firearms 1, Intimidation 4, Interrogation 2, Investigation 2, Linguistics 3 (English, Arabic, German, Russian), Rapport 1, Shadowing 1, Stealth 1, Streetwise 1, Subterfuge 2, Survival 1, Thought Discipline 3, Tradecraft 4

Backgrounds: Allies 4, Backing 5, Contacts 4, Equipment 6, Favors 5, Influence 5, Rank 6, Resources 3

Willpower 6

Lucas Barrows

Background: Raised in a close-knit neighborhood in the suburbs of Houston, Texas, Lucas Barrows grew up used to being above the norm. In his neighborhood, he was the tallest and best-looking kid. In his small public high school, he stayed at the top of his class. He even managed to letter in basketball, football and track for three consecutive years. He graduated valedictorian, was voted Most Likely to Succeed and received offers of full athletic and academic scholarships to several prominent colleges. The honors and accolades he achieved came to him almost without effort. Intent on a career in law-enforcement, Barrows accepted the University of Georgia's offer for a scholarship and enrolled in the Criminal Justice program.

And yet, as many young students do, Barrows learned that the characteristics that made him exceptional in public school were merely the norm in college. After a year, Barrows had to drop his extracurricular activities in order to keep up with his studies.

However, Barrows' interest in the prosecution of criminal law grew with every class he took. He graduated a respectable (if not spectacular) 30th in his class, with a minor in Psychology, and he exploited a connection he had made within the Georgia Bureau of Investigation through his undergraduate advisor. Within the year, he had acquired a job in the GBI as a criminal profiler.

Barrows spent the next 10 years in the same job, at the same desk, doing the same thing. One by one, he watched the stars of the GBI move on to positions within the Federal Bureau of Investigation, but he was unable to excel enough himself to move on.

Frustrated and stuck, Barrows took a short leave of absence. Retreating to his Atlanta apartment, he took stock of his life. His job paid enough money to support

ostentatious or flamboyant, even in high-profile social situations, such as dinners at the White House or the rare press conference.

Roleplaying Hints: You have your opinions, and you hold them in higher regard than most of the data your agents collect. You've been playing the intelligence game ever since your graduation from VMI, and you know the field better than many of your peers. You often come up with the best solution to any given problem first, and your assessment of a situation based on the data collected is usually the closest to the truth. Your common sense is often the only tool you need.

However, your knowledge of these facts does not always apply itself to the reality of functioning as a leader in the Directive. Rather than assuming that your common sense will prevail over the actions of your peers and subordinates, you realize that the world does not always work the way it should. That being the case, you are seldom surprised when events run counter to common sense. You accept that aspect of humanity, and you put your understanding of it to use as best you can.

As far as novas are concerned, you predict nothing but tragedy in humanity's future. Humanity's general lack of common sense, you realize, does not disappear upon eruption. You have no faith in the novas' ability to use their power wisely, nor do you have faith in the rest of humanity's ability to accept novas into human culture without serious upheaval. Even the Directive — a collection of the world's most powerful nations, all of which have a history of conflict with each other — is destined to fall prey to that same lack of sense.

But for as long as the Directive remains useful, you will remain connected to it. And as long as novas remain useful to the Directive, you will continue to use them as necessary. You are practical enough, however, to have already thought up a contingency against the day when the human and nova tendency to ignore common sense comes back to the fore on a worldwide scale.

nal Justice program offered him a standing invitation to be a guest lecturer whenever he had the time.

As his local fame grew and his reputation spread, his job performance only got better. Word of his skill finally spread to some of his former coworkers, and they recommended that Barrows apply to the FBI as they had. With no little prompting, they were able to convince Barrows that his long-unrecognized aptitude would be of better use at the federal level, rather than the state level. Barrows did as they suggested, and he turned his application in.

However, the interviewing and psychological-evaluation process revealed something Barrows had never suspected: His M-R node was active! The psychological stress he had been through and his attempted suicide had triggered an eruption. However, rather than giving him the power to fly or absorb fire, his eruption had given him the power to make his life better. Barrows accepted the FBI's offer of a job, and his local fame grew into national celebrity overnight. The very fact that his eruption had merely exaggerated his humanity (not to mention the fact that it had gone unnoticed for so long) made him something of a novelty among the burgeoning nova culture of the time. After only two more years of exemplary service to the FBI, Arnold Harris of the Directive offered Barrows the chance to be the first of his kind to join the multinational intelligence effort. Delighted to use his skills in an organization that did good work for the benefit of the entire world, rather than that of just one country, Barrows accepted Harris' offer and became the first nova agent on the Directive's payroll.

Image: Tall and good-looking, Barrows stands out in any crowd of baselines. He smiles often, and he deals good naturedly with his fellow agents. Now that he can afford it, he dresses in exquisitely tailored clothes on and off duty, and he never lets anyone see him ruffled. Lately, however, he's begun to grow somewhat withdrawn. While still radiant, his smile isn't quite as quick in coming as it once was. And more than once, janitors in the Directive's US headquarters have noticed Barrows leaving late at night with dark circles under his sparkling, intelligent eyes.

Roleplaying Hints: You're calm and in control at all times, if somewhat aloof. For some reason, it just isn't as easy to make friends with "baselines" now that people realize you've erupted. Sometimes, people look at you like they expect you to shoot fire from your eyes or fly off into the sky like a rocket. Or perhaps that look you see in their eyes is disappointment in the fact that you can't do those things. You've started noticing a similar expression on the faces of the novas you try to associate with.

Regardless, you do your job very well. You examine collected data on nova subjects and create profiles on them, just as you did for the Bureau. You also monitor operations from C3I while agents are in the field. Your insight on the novas around whom the operations revolve are invaluable to the missions' successful

him, although admittedly not in any grand style. He dated sporadically, but he had found no one special. He had few close friends at work or away from his job. He had made no discernible difference in the well-being of society, despite his desire to do so. In short, his life was leaving no real ripple in the world, regardless of how auspicious its beginning had seemed. As more time passed, thoughts of that nature continued to swirl around him, driving Barrows into a deep depression. He did not return to work, he ignored his parents' concerned phone calls, he refused to eat, and he even stopped bathing. The depression culminated in a breakdown that left Barrows lying on his bed between an empty bottle of Zoloft and a half-empty bottle of Jack Daniels.

Barrows awoke some indeterminate time later, much to his surprise. He smelled awful, his eyes were sunken and bloodshot, and his head was killing him, but he was still alive. As he staggered into his bathroom and offered the remnants of his failed suicide attempt to the toilet bowl, he experienced a revelation. He had been expecting his life to change and get better on its own, he realized, rather than making it better himself. Up until this point, he knew, he hadn't even had any idea *how* to make it better. But now he knew. Now he would get from life what he had expected to just come to him all along. Once his blinding headache finally went away, he returned to work at the GBI.

Psychological evaluations after his absence indicated that Barrows had, indeed, experienced a turnabout in his outlook on life. His job performance improved immensely, and even coworkers who had never said two words to him in the past 10 years could not help but notice how Barrows had taken a turn for the better. Within the year, his insights as a criminal profiler grew to legendary status within the Bureau. He briefly returned to the University of Georgia to turn his Psychology minor into a full-fledged degree, and the faculty of the Crimi-

resolutions. Without you — as your superiors assure you — field agents wouldn't know what they were up against.

Gear: The piece of equipment you rely on most is the personal computer in your office, from which you do your research and coordinate the operations of the agents who defer to you.

Nature: Gallant

Allegiance: Directive

Attributes: Strength 4, Dexterity 5, Stamina 5, Perception 5, Intelligence 5, Wits 4, Appearance 5, Manipulation 5, Charisma 4

Abilities: Academics 2, Analysis 3, Athletics 4, Awareness 5, Biz 3, Brawl 4, Bureaucracy 2, Command 3, Computer 3, Drive 4, Endurance 3, Etiquette 2, Firearms 3, Intimidation 3, Intrusion 1, Interrogation 3, Investigation 4, Legerdemain 1, Linguistics 3 (English, German, Japanese, Russian), Martial Arts 3, Melee 1, Might 3, Rapport 4, Resistance 3, Science 2, Shadowing 3, Stealth 1, Streetwise 2, Style 3, Subterfuge 3, Thought Discipline 4, Tradecraft 3

Backgrounds: Contacts 1, Dormancy 4, Equipment 2, Favors 2, Influence 2, Node 2, Rank 3, Resources 4

Quantum 1, Quantum Pool 22, Willpower 10, Taint 0

Powers: Mega-Intelligence • (Analyze Weakness), Mega-Manipulation • (Persuader), Intuition • • •, Luck • •, Psychic Shield • • •

Grayson Lorey

Background: Coming from a long, distinguished line of police officers in New York City, Grayson Lorey grew up with a unique understanding of the dynamics of police and criminal behavior. He spent his spare time with his father at the precinct, learning how the system worked and finding out what the job of a policeman was really like. Rather than applying directly to the police academy after high school, however, he turned his knowledge into a master's degree in Criminal Psychology at NYU.

Once he graduated college, he joined the police force as his family had been urging him to do ever since he graduated high school. Rather than remaining complacent as a patrolman, he made detective within a year, using his understanding of the criminal mind to good advantage. He was well on his way to the rank of captain when the first novas made international headlines. He himself sat dumbfounded in his car in the traffic jam that resulted from Randel Portman's dramatic eruption.

In the wake of that incident, Lorey took it upon himself to investigate Portman's background. What kind of man was this "Fireman"? And what kind of man had he become? Did he pose a threat to the citizens of New York? What steps would the NYPD have to take if such turned out to be the case? The profile he drew up in the course of his investigation was not of intelligence-professional caliber, but enough of his conclusions proved correct that he impressed his captain and caught the attention of the mayor himself. Taken in by the media hype of the nova phenomenon, the mayor, in turn, created a

special division of the force designed to handle "nova affairs" in the city.

Working with Project Utopia, the NYPD's nova division was designed to investigate crimes in which the victims and/or suspects were novas, to provide security for nova celebrities who visited the city and to report occurrences of recent eruptions to the staff at Project Utopia. Lorey headed the special division, establishing himself as a pioneer in the field of nova psychology as it related to crime and the law. Years later, when the Teragen movement took root in the city, it was Lorey to whom the mayor turned for advice.

Grayson's job, however, had become largely a sinecure in the time since Portman's eruption. Even though he commanded respect on the force, he was no longer able to advance in rank. Even though he performed an essential function in the NYPD nova division, he worked every day behind a desk, rather than out on the streets. He spent more time on the phone arranging meetings and acting as a consultant than he did visiting crime scenes and doing any real investigating. He asked for a transfer to Homicide or Narcotics, but his captain denied his request. He was too good at his job to be as useful anywhere else.

Therefore, when an offer came to him from former Deputy Director of the CIA Arnold Harris, asking him to consider joining a multinational organization designed to collect data on the effects of the Nova Age on the world at large, he jumped at the chance. Harris told him that both his experience as a detective and his experience in dealing with nova psychology made him a suitable candidate for training as a Directive operative. Harris even guaranteed Lorey frequent opportunities for field work once his training and evaluation period proved him to be capable of doing the job.

When the evaluation indeed proved such to be the case, Lorey resigned from the NYPD and relocated to

the Directive's US headquarters. He avoided an assignment to one of the Directive's public blue-and-white teams, attaching himself, instead, to the collection team that supported both Lucas Barrows and Jesse Hooks. In doing their jobs, the organization's two star nova agents relied on a wide array of complete, in-depth information on nova subjects, which Lorey and his team provided.

It eventually became Lorey's job to organize the data his team collected and make recommendations on what the data suggested about the subjects in question. Barrows used the information to create more complex psychological profiles from which he could extrapolate the subjects' future behavior; Hooks used the information to create convincing undercover identities for use in his infiltration operations. In short order, Lorey had impressed and befriended both Hooks and Barrows. Both novas trusted Lorey implicitly, as he did them. As he worked more closely with them, he began to drift farther away from field work and closer to being the novas' personal advisor and partner.

When Jesse Hooks defected to the Teragen cause, a thunderstruck Lorey gravitated even more closely to Lucas Barrows. The two maintain a close friendship, but Lorey can't help but wonder if (or when) Barrows' loyalty to his own kind will win out over his loyalty to the Directive as well.

Image: Still in his early 30s, Lorey dresses as casually as his job permits. He has his hair trimmed conservatively short, and he prefers glasses over contact lenses. His sedentary years on the force have left him slightly paunchy, but the training and activity he has been participating in as a Directive agent has begun to trim him back down.

Roleplaying Hints: Investigation in the field is what you live for. Your flair for armchair psychoanalysis is a useful tool, but that part of your job is not your favorite. You enjoy collecting first-hand data and piecing it together into a coherent form. On-site detective work is what you're really good at. You like to reconstruct motive, state of mind and circumstance from data you yourself collect. You can tell things about people just by observing them and the evidence of their passing. You're good at it. At least, that's what you've always thought.

You never questioned Hooks' loyalty, and you've taken his defection to the Teragen as a personal failure. Maybe if you hadn't been lulled into complacency behind your desk at the precinct, your instincts for that sort of thing wouldn't have been dulled. Your superiors have tried to convince you that Hooks suffered from a multiple-personality disorder that was exaggerated by his eruption and that you couldn't have predicted what he would have done, but you *knew* Hooks. That sort of thing shouldn't have gotten past you. It's your job not to let that sort of thing get past you.

Now, you've got your eye on Lucas Barrows. Barrows is your friend, he's good at what he does, and his loyalty seems beyond question, just as Hooks' did. You've

talked to Director Harris, and the two of you have agreed that Barrows should be watched more closely than ever before. After all, Barrows and Hooks were good friends. Should Barrows experience a similar change of heart, you'll be the one to root this out before it endangers the Directive. You won't fail again.

Gear: .45, belt-pack (with first-aid kit, mini-camera and eu-freeze canister), radio earpiece and laptop computer.
Nature: Judge
Allegiance: Directive
Attributes: Strength 2, Dexterity 2, Stamina 2, Perception 3, Intelligence 3, Wits 4, Appearance 2, Manipulation 3, Charisma 3
Abilities: Academics 2, Analysis 3, Awareness 2, Brawl 1, Bureaucracy 1, Command 1, Computer 2, Drive 1, Firearms 1, Endurance 2, Etiquette 1, Interrogation 3, Investigation 3, Linguistics 1, Rapport 3, Shadowing 1, Stealth 1, Streetwise 2, Subterfuge 1, Thought Discipline 1, Tradecraft 2,
Backgrounds: Allies 3, Backing 2, Contacts 3, Equipment 3, Favors 3, Mentor 1, Rank 4, Resources 3
Willpower 5

Anya Ilyanovich

Background: Growing up in Russia, Anya Ilyanovich had wanted nothing more than to dance for the Bolshoi. She pushed herself in dance classes and her hard work got results. She was lithe and graceful, and her every movement was dance embodied. Her future seemed assured. Unfortunately, as Anya matured and her talent developed, so did other parts of the young girl. Unlike her mother, who was a tiny, delicate flower, Anya developed into a voluptuous young woman. Anya soon saw her youthful potential begin to fade, weighed down by a cloak of heavy flesh. Depressed, she began to starve herself in an attempt to lose the weight and return to her earlier girlish shape. This initially seemed to work and Anya was convinced that she could still realize her dream if she could only master her appetite and dominate her body. Perhaps if her father hadn't been so caught up in his new position as Presidential Advisor or if her mother were still alive, someone might have realized what Anya was doing to herself before it was too late.

As it was, Anya became weak from her self-imposed starvation but redoubled her efforts in the dance studio with ever more demanding training regimens. Her failure in her training made her furious with herself, so she ate even less to punish herself. After flawlessly completing an extremely difficult routine in the studio one day (despite a tremendous headache), she passed out. Anya awakened in the hospital, astonished to find that the stress of her anorexia had caused her M-R node to erupt.

With her dreams of the Bolshoi forgotten, Anya gained the perspective to reexamine the life she had nearly thrown away. She concluded that if she were not meant for life in the ballet, then surely she was given

Nature: Martyr
Allegiance: Directive
Attributes: Strength 3, Dexterity 5, Stamina 4, Perception 3, Intelligence 3, Wits 5, Appearance 5, Manipulation 3, Charisma 4
Abilities: Arts 3, Athletics 4, Awareness 3, Bureaucracy 1, Computer 2, Drive 1, Endurance 3, Etiquette 1, Firearms 5, Interrogation 2, Intimidation 3, Intrusion 3, Investigation 3, Linguistics 2, Martial Arts 4, Melee 3, Might 2, Perform 4, Pilot 1, Resistance 3, Shadowing 3, Stealth 4, Streetwise 2, Style 4, Subterfuge 2, Thought Discipline 3, Tradecraft 3
Backgrounds: Allies 2, Backing 3, Cipher 3, Equipment 3, Favors 3, Mentor 4, Rank 3, Resources 2
Quantum 2, Quantum Pool 24, Willpower 6, Taint 0
Powers: Mega-Dexterity ●●● (Accuracy, Catfooted, Physical Prodigy), Mega-Perception ● (Electromagnetic Vision), Mega-Wits ● (Enhanced Initiative x 2, Quickness x 2)

Dr. Jacob Torbuld

Background: A noted psychologist, Dr. Torbuld was found by the Directive after he published a provocative paper on the nova mind. Jacob had been doing research on the stability of the human psyche. He wanted to discover how it coped with suddenly having massive amounts of power at its disposal. His methods were subjected to ridicule and investigated, in part due to his use of baselines.

In order to see the "power-twist" as he called it, Dr. Torbuld had taken ordinary citizens and, through pyrotechnics and psychotropic drugs, made them believe they had erupted. His findings were said to be unreliable because of the profound difference of the M-R node actually erupting and someone just thinking it had. But before he was shunned by the psychological community and the masses alike, he had managed to interview a number of active novas in the world: elites, Utopians and athletes alike.

this new lease on life for another purpose. Shortly thereafter, her father, Petr Ilyanovich, offered her a position within his nascent organization, explaining that there was much someone with her talents could do to make the world a better place. Anya agreed and became one of the first nova agents of the Directive, and the first from the RusCon.

Anya has since risen to a position of prominence within the organization. Unlike most agents, especially nova agents, Anya works alone (or with certain Directive-hired elites). Her specialties are infiltration and assassination. When "Petr's little girl" is called in, it is almost always because all other avenues have failed to resolve a situation and wetwork is now the only way to go. Anya in combat is a wonder to behold, a John Woo-esque bullet-ballet striking in its beauty and deadliness.

Image: Anya is a strikingly beautiful redhead who knows how to dress to impress. She makes heads turn at society functions and even on the battlefield, where she indulges an Emma Peel fashion sense to great effect with her skintight, leather outfits.

Roleplaying Notes: You are driven to succeed in the field just as you were in the ballet. You've fought alongside such luminaries as Totentanz and lived to talk about it. The only person in the Directive displeased with your performance is you. You can always think of ways a mission could have gone better, ways more lives might have been saved, and these thoughts push you to strive that much harder during the next assignment.

Gear: Twin Glock 9mm pistols, cannister of eufreeze, flash grenade and a variety of experimental devices such as EMP grenades, VTP dart guns and her trademark wrist grapple launchers (that can each fire a grappling hook with 100 feet of synthetic eufiber cable attached; while useful, only someone who has Accuracy such as Anya can consistently have the grapples go where she wants them; also makes a fine garrote in a pinch)

From these observations, he had developed a highly effective model of the nova mind, and its possibilities for taint, before the term was coined.

It was for this aspect of Torbuld's work that the Directive sought him out. Now he serves as one of the leaders of the Psy-Ops Division. His job is to evaluate novas, through his own methods and the intelligence gathered about them by Directive operatives. His data has been invaluable, and he has managed to predict the mental breakdowns of several active novas.

Unbeknownst to the Directive, the doctor is disgusted with the whole idea of novas, thinking of them as "primates with lighters". Beyond the data he turns over to his superiors, he keeps a series of secret files on novas detailing their psychological instabilities, mental conditions and suggestions on how they may be brought down. He often wonders if, somewhere in Utopia, another like-minded individual is doing the same thing and how much he is getting paid.

Image: Dr. Torbuld is a serious-minded scientist in his late 40s. When working in the lab, he wears the stereotypical white lab coat over a shirt and tie, but when venturing into the field, he finds his rapport with the clientele is much stronger if he goes for a less scientific look. Unfortunately, his attempts at more casual attire are stymied by his inability to grasp 21st century fashion trends.

Roleplaying Hints: You are a quiet man who doesn't tend to socialize, preferring to analyze data on personalities rather than having to interact with them. Nevertheless, you does have a small circle of fellow researchers and scientists you consort with on a regular basis. You would hesitate to call them friends, but you do enjoy their company and the debates that result from their particular viewpoints. Chief among these are fellow Directive agents Dr. Reinhard Heller and Sharon Li.

Gear: Access to moxinoquantamine, eclipsidol, sedatives and just about any other sort drug, experimental or not, that the Directive stocks

Nature: Analyst

Allegiance: Directive

Attributes: Strength 2, Dexterity 3, Stamina 1, Perception 4, Intelligence 4, Wits 2, Appearance 2, Manipulation 3, Charisma 2

Abilities: Academics 4, Analysis 5, Awareness 2, Biz 2, Bureaucracy 2, Command 2, Computer 4, Drive 2, Engineering 2, Intimidation 2, Investigation 3, Medicine 4, Rapport 3, Resistance 2, Science 4, Subterfuge 2

Backgrounds: Allies 2, Backing 3, Contacts 1, Influence 2, Resources 3

Willpower 3

Toshiro Yu

Background: Toshiro Yu has always been fascinated by language, not only his native Japanese but all languages. At a young age, he mastered the basics of both French and English, not because he was a linguistic prodigy, but out of sheer love for speech and its myriad of sounds. As

a young man, Yu followed many of his fellow language lovers into the theater. As a theater major, Yu's love of languages continued, with the young actor learning Chinese and its many variations. He became a popular local actor for his ability to perform the plays of other lands. But true success eluded him. Having gotten his degree, Yu went to Tokyo, expecting it to become the next Hollywood. However, fortune refused to favor him, as Mumbai became the next film capital of the world. He was forced to make his living teaching languages and soon became a highly sought after dialect coach, assisting those who had won the roles he himself wanted to play.

It was in this capacity that the Directive found him. One of their agents came to him, on recommendation, to learn French for an undercover assignment. Despite the fact that Yu had no knowledge of his student's life-or-death need to speak flawless French, his care and attention to detail enabled the assignment to go off without a hitch. As the years passed, Yu assisted several other agents without knowing of their clandestine activities, until the Directive decided to involve him personally.

Now Yu heads the language department of the Directive and flies all over the world assisting agents with their foreign accents and dialects. Furthermore, Yu's dreams of being an important actor have been partially realized. While natives to the East can tell an outsider just from his face, in the West, a gaijin can seldom tell a Japanese man from a Chinese man from a Burmese man. The Directive has utilized Yu's abilities by having him pose as anything from a business man who doesn't speak a word of English (and so can be talked in front of) to a waiter who can barely take an order, let alone collect organizational secrets for the Directive.

Image: Yu is an attractive man in his early 30s. He has been described as having a kind face. He does not have the looks of a movie star, but neither is he totally average. He fits in somewhere in the middle. And that is just where he wants to be. From this vantage, he can go to either end of the spectrum — being totally overlooked or causing quite a scene. He enjoys each immensely.

Roleplaying Hints: Though the Directive prefers to use you in a training capacity, you continually talk your way into operations because, frankly, you're the most qualified. You view each new field assignment as a chance to shine as an actor. Each of the characters in your repertoire is Oscar caliber. Too bad the only movie audience that will ever catch your performances is made up entirely of co-workers who review your cell's surveillance chips.

Gear: Makeup kit, bugs, one-time pad
Nature: Gallant
Allegiance: Directive
Attributes: Strength 2, Dexterity 3, Stamina 3, Perception 4, Intelligence 3, Wits 4, Appearance 3, Manipulation 4, Charisma 4
Abilities: Academics 2, Analysis 4, Arts 4, Athletics 2, Awareness 3, Biz 3, Brawl 2, Bureaucracy 2, Computer 2, Drive 2, Endurance 2, Etiquette 3, Firearms 2, Intrusion 2, Investigation 2, Legerdemain 3, Linguistics 8 (Japanese, Chinese - Manchurian, Mandarin and several regional dialects, Dutch, English, French, German, Russian, Spanish), Martial Arts 2, Perform 4, Rapport 3, Resistance 2, Stealth 2, Streetwise 2, Style 3, Thought Discipline 2
Backgrounds: Allies 2, Backing 4, Cipher 2, Contacts 2, Equipment 1, Resources 2
Willpower 3

Dr. Reinhard Heller

Background: When he finally decided to commit to a university, Reinhard Heller chose Sociology and Psychology as his fields of studies. It was at this same time that novas began their rise to prominence, and through

them, Heller was presented with a unique opportunity. A new field of study had suddenly opened up, a new force of nature driven by the human personality. Heller became one of the first students to sign up for the new field of Quantum Studies and the first to graduate with doctorate in it from his university.

It was in his subsequent post-doctoral work interviewing novas to come up with correlations between the stress of eruption and the form quantum manipulation abilities take that he met and became friends with Dr. Jacob Torbuld. At first bitter rivals, the men found themselves agreeing on many theoretical conclusions. And so it was after Torbuld's fall from grace, and subsequent soft landing, that the first name on his list of associates to be recruited by the Directive was Reinhard Heller.

The two work on separate projects for the Directive in separate parts of the world, but communicate via OpNet weekly with their findings. They also stay in contact through Sharon Li, a nova whose abilities are used and researched by both men. Reinhard continues his studies of eruption, and how the personality affects what type of quantum powers novas have but also added his experience to Dr. Torbuld's ongoing project on the prediction and manipulation of eruption, a topic that is most intriguing to both men.

Image: Dr. Heller doesn't look like a doctor. He refrains from the traditional trappings of his profession. He wears shorts almost constantly, at any time of the year. He is a jovial fellow, quick with a joke or a smile.

Roleplaying Notes: Many who first begin their work with you doubt your abilities and wonder if you have ever even been to college, much less earned a doctorate. That is, until they begin to question your conclusions. Then they get to see the full fury of your intelligence in the form of a seething torrent of facts and figures that can reduce even the most egotistical of scientists into meek submission.

Gear: Spiral notebook, chip recorder, hacky-sack
Nature: Visionary
Allegiance: Directive
Attributes: Strength 2, Dexterity 3, Stamina 3, Perception 3, Intelligence 5, Wits 4, Appearance 3, Manipulation 4, Charisma 4
Abilities: Academics 3, Analysis 2, Arts 2, Awareness 3, Biz 2, Brawl 1, Bureaucracy 2, Command 3, Computer 4, Drive 1, Engineering 2, Intimidation 2, Investigation 3, Linguistics 1 (German, English), Medicine 4, Perform 2, Rapport 3, Science 4, Style 3, Subterfuge 2
Backgrounds: Allies 2, Backing 4, Contacts 2, Favors 3, Influence 1, Resources 2
Willpower 3

Sharon Li

Background: Sharon Li was a waitress on her way home from work when she stumbled into a gang war. The two rival factions, both led by novas, were attacking each other in the street while their leaders were brawled in the sky. One was shooting energy from his hands, trying in

vain to hit his faster and much more agile opponent. A loud, electric crack came from above and Li saw the smaller of the fighters catch a blast in the face and come careening down toward one of the buildings framing a basketball court. He collided with the building, sending large chunks of brick and mortar raining down to street level. The nova had crashed near where a group of children were huddled on the court. Li's head began pounding with rage. Something snapped inside of Li, and she ran over, grabbed a hunk of brick and hurled it at the fleeing nova.

It was an accurate throw. The rock collided with the back of the flying man's head. He barely acknowledged with the impact, but spun around in mid-air, incredulous that someone had assaulted him. And he found a young Asian woman standing in the center of the street, still in her white and blue waitressing uniform, holding another chunk of brick in her hand. None of the witnesses heard what was said between the two, but the intent was clear. The nova's eyes glowed brightly as his face contorted in anger. He reached back and hurled a bolt of white energy at the young woman, intent on incinerating her.

Li was as surprised as the nova when she caught the bolt and threw it right back at him. The energy knocked him back a few feet, but the look on his face said the act was what had done the real damage. He was beginning to charge another blast, when he cocked his head to one side, and seemed to be listening down the street. He looked back at Li, sneered and headed back to rejoin his troops. A few minutes later, sirens were heard as nova-assisted police officers responded to the chaos. Li had remained motionless all the while, glaring in the direction of the nova's retreat. She stood there until an officer asked if she was all right. The moment he touched her arm, Li collapsed and fell into a coma that lasted for three days.

She was treated as an newly erupted nova, but no one was able to determine what her powers were. She didn't manifest any nova abilities during the rest of her stay in the hospital or over the next few weeks at home. She returned to work, and dealt with her brush with fame, as "The woman who told El Tenedor 'No More!'" But her fame passed, and her life continued as always until Dr. Heller showed up at her door.

Dr. Reinhard Heller told her that she had actually become a nova, one that could duplicate the powers of others. The only powers that she had were the ones of novas around her. Li was doubtful, but liked the doctor and agreed to travel with him to help with his research. Just as in the street, when Li came in close proximity to another nova, she gained his powers. It was then that Li quit her job and joined the Directive — though as Dr. Heller's assistant, not as a nova operative.

Image: Sharon Li was a very attractive woman even before the eruption. The quantum energies in her body have only made her more so. But she is only now learning to use her appearance to her advantage, either dressing up or down depending on the situation. The only major caveat being that she not appear as a nova. Her true nature is concealed from the majority of people, and her appearance reflects her supposedly mundane self. Li is in her late 20s and has long dark hair and light brown skin. When not "in costume," she prefers baggy clothes that don't restrict her movement. When she is on the job, she can range from dynamic to dull or anything in between.

Roleplaying Notes: You travel with both Dr. Heller and Dr. Torbuld on their trips to meet and interview novas. Through their experiments, you have gained a better understanding of your own powers and experienced a wide variety of the powers and abilities exhibited by others.

On occasion, you have worked as an operative on covert teams whose objectives are to discover and catalogue the unknown abilities of a number of novas, but for the most part, you work with the two doctors detailing to them what you can about the novas you meet.

Gear: Notepad, pen, cell phone

Nature: Follower

Allegiance: Directive

Attributes: Strength 2, Dexterity 4, Stamina 4, Perception 5, Intelligence 3, Wits 4, Appearance 4, Manipulation 3, Charisma 3

Abilities: Academics 3, Analysis 1, Arts 3, Athletics 2, Awareness 4, Biz 2, Brawl 2, Bureaucracy 2, Command 2, Computer 2, Drive 2, Endurance 3, Etiquette 2, Firearms 2, Intimidation 1, Intrusion 1, Investigation 3, Linguistics 2 (English, Chinese, German), Martial Arts 2, Medicine 2, Perform 2, Rapport 3, Resistance 2, Science 2, Stealth 2, Streetwise 2, Style 3, Subterfuge 2, Survival 2, Tradecraft 2

Backgrounds: Allies 3, Attunement 2, Backing 4, Cipher 2, Contacts 3, Dormancy 4, Equipment 1, Favors 1, Influence 1, Mentor 3, Node 2, Rank 2, Resources 2

Quantum 4, Quantum Pool 28, Willpower 6, Taint 2

Powers: Quantum Leech ● ● ● ● ●

Templates
Shadow

When you were born, Berlin was a city split in two. Eighteen years later, the wall came tumbling down, just in time to ruin your dreams of being a spy for the West. Your mother always said that the only reason you learned English was so you could read English spy novels in the original tongue. She was probably right. Fleming, Forsythe, Le Carre, even Clancy. You grew up knowing more about dead-letter drops and one-time pads than a career man at MI6, or so you thought.

With the end of the Cold War, the intelligence business lost much of its allure. By the time you graduated from college, all anyone cared about was Middle Eastern terrorists and satellite imagery. So instead of becoming a spy, you became a cop. Not quite the same, but at least it had some of the same exciting qualities as spy work did. You tried undercover work for a while and found it rewarding but not ultimately satisfying. You transferred over to the Berlin domestic-terrorist task force, aimed at skinheads and scientologists for the most part. As it turns out, your timing was perfect. It was 1998.

A year later, Berlin was having its first problems with nova anarchists — super-powered punks who roamed the streets at night, smashing Jewish and foreign owned storefronts by tossing police cars through them. Your group got the job of bringing these quantum-powered menaces to justice. You led the cell, found a probable suspect and followed him for five days before you had enough proof to make an arrest. Then you helped take him down, along with some novas from Project Utopia who flew in at the last minute to "consult" and, as it turns out, take the credit.

Even within the department, your efforts went largely unrecognized. However, the nova craze had caught you just like everyone else. The only difference was, while most people viewed novas as heroes, you saw them as a challenge and maybe a danger. The nova menace in Berlin, and later Munich and

Dresden where you set up other nova-control task forces, excited and stimulated you the same way you always dreamed spying on the East Germans would have. You quietly made a name for yourself as a nova hunter, a man who could sniff out any quantum-powered criminal in the city. Despite your success, promotion and recognition from above eluded you. Rumor had it that you'd somehow angered Project Utopia and that they were working against you. You doubted it though. You simply weren't that important.

Then they fired you. You're still not sure why. Ostensibly, they let you go because of budget cuts. Possibly, they had other reasons, other pressures bearing down on them. You'll probably never know for sure, but at this point, it doesn't matter anymore. A week later you had a new job, working for a private security firm and making twice the money for half the work. This new job still focused on novas, although now you were merely gathering information on them as opposed to investigating criminal activities. No one told you what they used the data for, although they hinted that it had something to do with a nova watchdog group of some sort.

What you couldn't have known at the time was that you were actually part of the first operational cell the German government set up as part of its new membership in the Directive. After three months, you were "promoted" and sent off for some special training. That's when you joined the Directive for real. You'd heard about the group, even used some Directive-produced training material while working for the police. This was your childhood dream come true: You would actually become a spy, working against an enemy as dangerous and crafty as the East German Stasi ever was. You haven't looked back since.

Image: In your early 40s, of average height and medium build, with no distinguishing features, you typically wear whatever clothes will augment your already extraordinary ability to blend seamlessly into any group.

Roleplaying Notes: Your job is to blend in with the background. You specialize in following novas (or normal people) for days at a time without them ever growing suspicious. This talent for blending in exists within your own personality as well. Basically a quiet, reserved person, you are also a social chameleon. You can fit into any crowd, get along with anyone. At the same time, you don't make much of an impression after you've left. You laugh at others' jokes but tell none of your own. You agree with the majority and don't voice any memorable opinions. All the while, you watch everything, taking it in and locking it away in your mind until you need to use it. It might not make you a hit with the ladies, but it does give you an edge against novas.

Gear: Appropriate to your current assignment

ABERRANT CHARACTER SHEET

Birth Name: Shadow
Code Name:
Series:

Eruption:
Nature: Analyst
Allegiance: Directive

ATTRIBUTES AND ABILITIES

PHYSICAL

STRENGTH ●●○○○
Brawl ○○○○○
Might ○○○○○
_____ ○○○○○

DEXTERITY ●●●○○
Athletics ○○○○○
Drive ●●●○○
Firearms ●●○○○
Legerdemain ○○○○○
MartialArts ○○○○○
Melee ○○○○○
Pilot ○○○○○
Stealth ●●●●○
_____ ○○○○○
_____ ○○○○○

STAMINA ●●●○○
Endurance ○○○○○
Resistance ○○○○○
_____ ○○○○○
_____ ○○○○○

MENTAL

PERCEPTION ●●●●○
Awareness ○○○○○
Investigation ○○○○○
_____ ○○○○○

INTELLIGENCE ●●●○○
Analysis ○○○○○
Bureaucracy ○○○○○
Computer ○○○○○
Engineering ○○○○○
Intrusion ●●●●●
Linguistics ○○○○○
Medicine ○○○○○
Science ○○○○○
Survival ○○○○○
Tradecraft ●●●○○

WITS ●●●○○
Arts ○○○○○
Rapport ○○○○○
Shadowing ●●●●●
Thought Discipline ●●●○○

SOCIAL

APPEARANCE ●●○○○
Intimidation ○○○○○
Style ○○○○○
_____ ○○○○○

MANIPULATION ●●○○○
Interrogation ○○○○○
Streetwise ○○○○○
Subterfuge ○○○○○
_____ ○○○○○
_____ ○○○○○
_____ ○○○○○

CHARISMA ●●○○○
Command ○○○○○
Etiquette ○○○○○
Perform ○○○○○
_____ ○○○○○
_____ ○○○○○
_____ ○○○○○
_____ ○○○○○

ADVANTAGES

BACKGROUNDS

Cipher ●●●○○
Resources ●●○○○
Favors ●●○○○
Equipment ●●○○○
Rank ●●○○○
Contacts ●●○○○

WILLPOWER
●●●●○○○○○○
□□□□□□□□□□

TAINT
○○○○○○○○○○
□□□□□□□□□□

ABERRATIONS
_____
_____
_____

QUANTUM
○○○○○○○○○○

MEGA-ATTRIBUTES
_____ ○○○○○
_____ ○○○○○
_____ ○○○○○
_____ ○○○○○
_____ ○○○○○
_____ ○○○○○
_____ ○○○○○
_____ ○○○○○
_____ ○○○○○
_____ ○○○○○
_____ ○○○○○
_____ ○○○○○

QUANTUM POWERS
_____ ○○○○○
_____ ○○○○○
_____ ○○○○○
_____ ○○○○○
_____ ○○○○○
_____ ○○○○○
_____ ○○○○○
_____ ○○○○○
_____ ○○○○○

QUANTUM POOL
○○
□□

Cell Leader

You've been with the Directive since the beginning. In fact, you represent one of the rarer types of operative in the entire organization: someone who has never known any other kind of work. When you graduated from university in Petrograd, Russia was a nation in turmoil. The economy was rotten, mobsters ran the cities, and jobs were scarce. You had served two years in military intelligence before heading off to school where you majored in International Politics. The first eruptions of novas came during your third year at school. Like most people around the world, these amazing individuals fascinated you. You chose "The Impact of Novas on World Politics" as your thesis topic.

Working on the research, talking to nova "experts" around the world, you learned a lot about novas and came to feel that they represented quite a threat. These quantum-powered beings could totally destroy the balance of power in international relations. They represented a force as unstable and deadly as nuclear weapons. More dangerous, in fact, because at least nuclear weapons required skill and money to build and could not think for themselves. You published your findings online, but few people took notice. Fortunately, an American-Russian policy think tank did see it and offered you a grant to continue your research.

Over the next year and a half, you wrote four more papers and even hired a few assistants to help you gather data on eruptions throughout Russia and the former Soviet states. What no one realized, not even the people paying for it, was that you and your group would someday become one of the first Directive cells in Russia. When the Russian Confederation, the United States, Japan and Great Britain joined together to form the Directive as a counter to the growing nova threat, they came to you as a potential member. Although you had no idea what you were getting yourself into at the time, you readily agreed. It didn't hurt that your funding was running out.

In those early days, during your period at the Black Sea training dacha, you were as much a teacher as a pupil. You lectured to fellow students about the policy implications of individual novas and their powers, while the Directive taught you how to be a spy.

Six months later, after the most rigorous work you'd ever done, your cell went operational — the first in Moscow. Your job then was simply to watch and learn all you could about the city's novas. It was much the same thing you'd done as a researcher and academic, only now you had government backing, bugs, wiretaps and a team of talented spies at your disposal. You helped set up several sub-cells within the city as well, discreet teams that worked under your direction. Soon, you had every nova in the city wired and monitored around-the-clock.

Then you requested a transfer. More than anything, you like a challenge. You and your new cell were one of the first to operate outside a Directive member nation, in this case Turkey. You ran the only cell in the whole country, facings the challenges of both keeping an eye on the local novas (and in one case taking a dangerous nova out) and, at the same time, eluding detection by the local authorities. You worked there for two years, and although you had some setbacks, overall, your record shows distinction and success. You followed that effort with a series of similar assignments, working in countries as varied as Somalia, Indonesia and Italy.

Your talent and friends within the Directive could have let you rise into the ranks of the administration. In fact, you spent some time training other operatives back in the Crimea before requesting a transfer to operational status once again. You've become a bit of an adrenaline junkie and aren't happy unless you're leading a cell against a nova. Part of this is thrill seeking, but most of it stems from the fact that novas continue to become more populous and more dangerous than ever before. Russia and the world need your skills in the field.

Image: In your mid-30s, your prematurely graying hair and conservative style of dress give you an appearance of maturity that makes leading your cell that much easier.

Roleplaying Notes: You are a gregarious, pleasant person. You lead your cells like an amiable older sister when you can, seldom raising your voice or losing your temper. When you give an order, often as not, you phrase it as a request. Of course, it's not a request, and new recruits quickly learn to do what you say, when you say it. Experience has taught you that the work environment of a cell must be pleasant but controlled. No one should feel undue pressure from within the cell because there is plenty coming from the outside. Your troops do a good job because they know you'll be disappointed in them if they don't, not because they fear your reprisals. You work much the same way with your own superiors and other cell leaders (the few you know anyway). You foster strong interpersonal relationships and rely on them rather than rank and regulations to get things done.

Gear: 9mm Glock, cell phone with built-in MNG, canister of eu-freeze

ABERRANT CHARACTER SHEET

Birth Name: Cell Leader
Code Name:
Series:

Eruption:
Nature: Bureaucrat
Allegiance: Directive

ATTRIBUTES AND ABILITIES

PHYSICAL

STRENGTH ●●○○○
Brawl ○○○○○
Might ○○○○○
○○○○○

DEXTERITY ●●○○○
Athletics ○○○○○
Drive ○○○○○
Firearms ○○○○○
Legerdemain ○○○○○
MartialArts ○○○○○
Melee ○○○○○
Pilot ○○○○○
Stealth ○○○○○
○○○○○
○○○○○

STAMINA ●●○○○
Endurance ○○○○○
Resistance ○○○○○
○○○○○
○○○○○

MENTAL

PERCEPTION ●●●○○
Awareness ●○○○○
Investigation ○○○○○
○○○○○

INTELLIGENCE ●●●●○
Analysis ○○○○○
Bureaucracy ●●○○○
Computer ●○○○○
Engineering ○○○○○
Intrusion ○○○○○
Linguistics ●●○○○
Medicine ○○○○○
Science ○○○○○
Survival ○○○○○
Tradecraft ●●○○○

WITS ●●●○○
Arts ○○○○○
Rapport ●●●○○
Shadowing ○○○○○
Thought Discipline ●●○○○

SOCIAL

APPEARANCE ●●●○○
Intimidation ●●○○○
Style ○○○○○
○○○○○

MANIPULATION ●●●●○
Interrogation ●●●○○
Streetwise ○○○○○
Subterfuge ○○○○○
○○○○○
○○○○○
○○○○○
○○○○○

CHARISMA ●●●●○
Command ●●●●●
Etiquette ○○○○○
Perform ○○○○○
○○○○○
○○○○○
○○○○○
○○○○○

ADVANTAGES

BACKGROUNDS

Allies ●●○○○
Contacts ●●●○○
Equipment ●●●○○
Favors ●●●●●
Influence ●●○○○
Rank ●●●●○

WILLPOWER
●●●○○○○○○○
□□□□□□□□□□

TAINT
○○○○○○○○○○
□□□□□□□□□□

ABERRATIONS
_____
_____
_____

QUANTUM
○○○○○○○○○○

MEGA-ATTRIBUTES

_____ ○○○○○
_____ ○○○○○
_____ ○○○○○
_____ ○○○○○
_____ ○○○○○
_____ ○○○○○
_____ ○○○○○
_____ ○○○○○
_____ ○○○○○
_____ ○○○○○
_____ ○○○○○
_____ ○○○○○

QUANTUM POWERS

_____ ○○○○○
_____ ○○○○○
_____ ○○○○○
_____ ○○○○○
_____ ○○○○○
_____ ○○○○○
_____ ○○○○○
_____ ○○○○○
_____ ○○○○○
_____ ○○○○○

QUANTUM POOL

○○
□□

Counter-Nova Specialist

Very few novas work for the Directive. As far as most of your kind are concerned, a nova working for the Directive is like a Jew working for the Nazis. As far as you're concerned, most of your kind can go straight to hell. Erupting changes a person, a fact you know as well as any nova. The power rush, the feeling that anything is possible, the desire to stretch your powers to their limit, all these things change a man. The change is seldom for the better.

You nearly lost control yourself. If you'd had violent powers you probably would have killed someone. As it was, you caused plenty of harm to your friends, family and a number of luckless strangers. Your powers are literally all in your head. You're smarter than 99.9% of the geniuses out there and notice things most people couldn't see if they knew what to look for. This great big, quantum-powered brain of yours made you cocky, full of yourself. You pushed "baselines" away, seeking friends among "your own kind." You used your abilities, not too spectacular by nova standards, to abuse and exploit normal humans. Everything from playing the stock market to gambling to confidence schemes. You did it just to prove that you could.

This went on for about a year, and then you had the presence of mind to turn that amazing intellect back upon its owner. You realized just how fatuous it all was, how much of a jerk you'd become. It didn't take long to realize that you weren't the only one. All of your nova acquaintances were just like you. Even the so-called heroes and "good guys" were so full of themselves and their own abilities that it made you sick. You could see all too clearly how dangerous quantum powers really were. Even though Project Utopia was supposed to train novas how to use their powers wisely, they weren't doing anything to train them to control their pride.

You started to speak out against what you saw as wrong with novas in England and abroad. Being a nova yourself — albeit not a very sexy one — you even managed to get some air time on N! and the major OpNet chats. You're not sure if you convinced anyone, but you sure made some enemies. One of them, a nova named Beastly Jack, showed up at your house one morning and busted down the door. All your intellect and the shotgun in your hand weren't about to do you much good against this brute, an acknowledged Teragen adherent and outspoken critic of anything finding fault with novakind.

As luck would have it, Jack had a few fans he never knew about, a Directive cell that had been watching him and you. They stepped in before he could seriously hurt you, immobilizing and arresting him before the bastard knew what hit him. Then they offered you sanctuary, a hidden life away from the increasingly hostile company of novas like Jack. You accepted.

You haven't met another nova since, although you've watched plenty of them from afar. You work with cells all over Western Europe, analyzing and coordinating efforts against the Teragen, Project Utopia and other nova threats. Your keen intellect can sort through reams of data and seek out a nova's weak point. You're the Directive equivalent of a criminal profiler. Through logic, observation and deduction, you can tell more about a nova than he knows about himself. But that's only half the fun. Once you've come up with the profile, then you get to come up with a plan to bring the target down. You particularly enjoy psychological ploys, the kind of attack no nova, no matter what their powers, can resist for long. Everyone has feelings, worries and hopes. Your job is to turn them against a person.

Image: You're rather plain looking for a nova. When not in uniform, the clothing you wear invariably reflects your blue-collar upbringing. Your most striking features are a pair of piercing blue eyes that reveal an immense depth of intellegence to those who meet your gaze.

Roleplaying Notes: You grew up in Liverpool, a lower-middle class kid, unexceptional in every way. Even now that you're one of the smartest people on the planet, you still hold onto your working class roots and attitudes. You curse, you laugh, and you don't take crap from anyone. The more you work with the Directive, the more you despise novas in general, although you have too much self-confidence to transfer that disgust to yourself. You're done feeling sorry for yourself and view your work as a way to give back to the world after taking from it for so long. For all your bluster and "hardness," you're actually a very responsible, civic minded person. Just don't let anyone know it.

Gear: Notebook computer with OpNet, cell phone, shotgun

ABERRANT CHARACTER SHEET

Birth Name: Counter-Nova Specialist
Code Name:
Series:

Eruption:
Nature: Critic
Allegiance: Directive

ATTRIBUTES AND ABILITIES

PHYSICAL

STRENGTH ●●○○○
Brawl ____ ○○○○○ □
Might ____ ○○○○○ □
____ ○○○○○ □

DEXTERITY ●●○○○
Athletics ____ ○○○○○ □
Drive ____ ○○○○○ □
Firearms ____ ○○○○○ □
Legerdemain ____ ○○○○○ □
MartialArts ____ ○○○○○ □
Melee ____ ○○○○○ □
Pilot ____ ○○○○○ □
Stealth ____ ○○○○○ □
____ ○○○○○ □
____ ○○○○○ □

STAMINA ●●○○○
Endurance ____ ○○○○○ □
Resistance ____ ○○○○○ □
____ ○○○○○ □
____ ○○○○○ □

MENTAL

PERCEPTION ●●●●●
Awareness ____ ●●●●○ □
Investigation ____ ●●●●● □
____ ○○○○○ □

INTELLIGENCE ●●●●●
Analysis ____ ●●●●○ □
Bureaucracy ____ ○○○○○ □
Computer ____ ○○○○○ □
Engineering ____ ○○○○○ □
Intrusion ____ ○○○○○ □
Linguistics ____ ○○○○○ □
Medicine ____ ○○○○○ □
Science ____ ○○○○○ □
Survival ____ ○○○○○ □
Tradecraft ____ ●●●●○ □

WITS ●●●○○
Arts ____ ○○○○○ □
Rapport ____ ○○○○○ □
Shadowing ____ ○○○○○ □
Thought Discipline ●●○○○ □

SOCIAL

APPEARANCE ●●○○○
Intimidation ____ ●●○○○ □
Style ____ ○○○○○ □
____ ○○○○○ □

MANIPULATION ●●●○○
Interrogation ____ ●●●●○ □
Streetwise ____ ●○○○○ □
Subterfuge ____ ●○○○○ □
____ ○○○○○ □
____ ○○○○○ □
____ ○○○○○ □

CHARISMA ●●●○○
Command ____ ○○○○○ □
Etiquette ____ ○○○○○ □
Perform ____ ○○○○○ □
____ ○○○○○ □
____ ○○○○○ □
____ ○○○○○ □

ADVANTAGES

BACKGROUNDS
Cipher ____ ●●●○○
Dormancy ____ ●●●○○
Favors ____ ●●●○○
Mentor ____ ●●○○○
Rank ____ ●○○○○
Resources ____ ●●○○○

WILLPOWER
●●●●●●○○○○
□□□□□□□□□□

TAINT
○○○○○○○○○○
□□□□□□□□□□

ABERRATIONS
____
____
____

QUANTUM
●●○○○○○○○○

MEGA-ATTRIBUTES
Mega-Perception ____ ●●●○○
(Electromagnetic Vision)
Mega-Intelligence ____ ●●●○○
(Analyze Weakness, Mental Prodigy – Investigative)
____ ○○○○○
____ ○○○○○
____ ○○○○○
____ ○○○○○
____ ○○○○○
____ ○○○○○
____ ○○○○○
____ ○○○○○
____ ○○○○○
____ ○○○○○

QUANTUM POWERS
____ ○○○○○
____ ○○○○○
____ ○○○○○
____ ○○○○○
____ ○○○○○
____ ○○○○○
____ ○○○○○
____ ○○○○○
____ ○○○○○
____ ○○○○○

QUANTUM POOL
●●●●●●●●●●●●●●●●●●●●●●●●●●●●○○○○○○○○○○○○
□□

Nova Mole

They say folks get what they deserve. More to the point, they say that a nova's quantum abilities reflect her personality. That's certainly true in your case, whether by luck or design. You've always had a penchant for looking into other people's business, "poking your nose where it doesn't belong" as your mother often said. When you headed off to college in Chicago, away from your parents and the restrictions of small town life, you really let yourself go wild. You lost your first roommate because you read her diary. You got kicked out of the dorms the next year for breaking into the RA's room. You just wanted to look around, you weren't going to take anything.

It was during your appearance before the disciplinary council that you erupted, although no one knew it at the time. All of a sudden, it sounded like everyone in the room was shouting at once, except they had their mouths closed. It was their minds that were shouting at you, and suddenly you could hear them. You managed to make it through the meeting but said little in your defense. You spent the rest of the day wandering around campus in a daze, overwhelmed, but intrigued, by the voices.

Eventually, the voices faded away. Hearing them now required you to concentrate, which was just as well, since you're pretty sure you'd have gone insane otherwise. You'd seen plenty of N! in your day and read up on telepathy. Apparently, most folks knew when they were being scanned by a telepathic nova, but no one knew when you used your power. Interesting. All the literature encouraged novas to join Project Utopia, to get help with their problems. You were never much of a Team Tomorrow fan and decided your abilities served you better if no one knew about them.

For the next year, you were like a kid in a candy store. You dropped out of school and used your power to have fun. All kinds of fun. You made money gambling, you amazed your friends with your knowledge and insight, you seduced men who would never have given you the time of day if you hadn't known exactly what they wanted to hear. Somewhere along the line, you slipped up, let on more than you had intended. The Directive had figured out who and what you were.

As it turned out, that was a good thing. Despite what people say, the Directive agents that approached you weren't sinister or fascist. They were friendly, although, rather annoyingly, you found that you couldn't read their minds. All you got were nursery rhymes and math equations. They offered to train you, to show you how you could use your powers to achieve more than you ever dreamed of. Yeah, yeah, yeah, sounded just like the basic Project Utopia line of bull. No, no they said, not at all. You'd have access to secrets, things no one else knows. Then they told you some of those secrets, stuff about Utopia that somehow never makes it to N! or the front pages. You knew they were playing you, but it didn't matter. They had found your weakness: the need to know.

You trained for a long time, it was harder than anything you'd ever done before in your life, but it was all really interesting. As it turned out, they were training you for something very special, something uniquely suited to your abilities. You knew you were going to be a spy, but when they gave you the assignment you couldn't believe it. You were going to be a mole, a double agent planted within the ranks of Project Utopia itself. It was all too perfect. The Directive taught you how to use your telepathy like most mind-readers — so people would feel it when you scanned them. That way no one would suspect you could also read their minds without them being aware of it. They also trained you in plenty of normal spy stuff too, like planting bugs, hacking computers and picking locks.

Then they staged a very public eruption for you, right in a busy mall. You recreated your original feelings, but instead of keeping quiet you ran around yelling and screaming, violently touching nearby minds and generally making a huge scene. Project Utopia called the next day. Ever since then you've been a wolf in the fold, learning all you can and passing it on to your Directive handlers. Thus far, you haven't gotten any stellar material but you hope to fix that soon.

Image: You are a moderately attractive American woman of Asian descent. You tend to dress somewhat flamboyantly to play up your "flake psychic" image.

Roleplaying Notes: Although naturally quiet and reserved, as a mole you play the role of the slightly hysterical young woman. You try to make people underestimate you emotionally and intellectually but still respect you for your abilities. You need to appear competent enough within Utopia to rise through the ranks but not so much that you stand out. You also make friends very easily, or at least pretend friends. Surreptitiously reading minds, you tell people exactly what they want to hear, winning over their confidence and affection with ease. You have plenty of Utopia "friends", none of whom you like in the least. You can't wait for the day when you can bust the whole thing wide open. Some people might call that meanspirited. You call it doing your job and having fun at the same time.

Gear: CompReader, one-time pad

ABERRANT CHARACTER SHEET

Birth Name: Nova Mole
Code Name:
Series:

Eruption:
Nature: Explorer
Allegiance: Directive

ATTRIBUTES AND ABILITIES

PHYSICAL

STRENGTH ●●○○○
- Brawl ○○○○○
- Might ○○○○○
- ___ ○○○○○

DEXTERITY ●●○○○
- Athletics ○○○○○
- Drive ○○○○○
- Firearms ○○○○○
- Legerdemain ○○○○○
- MartialArts ○○○○○
- Melee ○○○○○
- Pilot ○○○○○
- Stealth ●●○○○
- ___ ○○○○○
- ___ ○○○○○

STAMINA ●●○○○
- Endurance ○○○○○
- Resistance ○○○○○
- ___ ○○○○○
- ___ ○○○○○

MENTAL

PERCEPTION ●●●○○
- Awareness ●●●○○
- Investigation ●●●○○
- ___ ○○○○○

INTELLIGENCE ●●●○○
- Analysis ○○○○○
- Bureaucracy ○○○○○
- Computer ○○○○○
- Engineering ○○○○○
- Intrusion ●●●○○
- Linguistics ○○○○○
- Medicine ○○○○○
- Science ○○○○○
- Survival ○○○○○
- Tradecraft ●●●●●

WITS ●●●●●
- Arts ○○○○○
- Rapport ○○○○○
- Shadowing ○○○○○
- Thought Discipline ●●●○○

SOCIAL

APPEARANCE ●●○○○
- Intimidation ○○○○○
- Style ○○○○○
- ___ ○○○○○

MANIPULATION ●●●●○
- Interrogation ○○○○○
- Streetwise ○○○○○
- Subterfuge ●●●●●
- ___ ○○○○○
- ___ ○○○○○

CHARISMA ●●○○○
- Command ○○○○○
- Etiquette ○○○○○
- Perform ●●●○○
- ___ ○○○○○
- ___ ○○○○○
- ___ ○○○○○

ADVANTAGES

BACKGROUNDS

- Backing ●●●○○
- Cipher ●●●●●
- Favors ●●●○○
- Rank ●○○○○
- Resources ●●○○○
- ___ ○○○○○

WILLPOWER
●●●●●●●●○○
□□□□□□□□□□

TAINT
○○○○○○○○○○
□□□□□□□□□□

ABERRATIONS
___
___
___

QUANTUM
●●●○○○○○○○

MEGA-ATTRIBUTES
- ___ ○○○○○
- ___ ○○○○○
- ___ ○○○○○
- ___ ○○○○○
- ___ ○○○○○
- ___ ○○○○○
- ___ ○○○○○
- ___ ○○○○○
- ___ ○○○○○
- ___ ○○○○○
- ___ ○○○○○
- ___ ○○○○○
- ___ ○○○○○

QUANTUM POWERS
- Telepathy ●●●○○
  (Surreptitious)
- ___ ○○○○○
- ___ ○○○○○
- ___ ○○○○○
- ___ ○○○○○
- ___ ○○○○○
- ___ ○○○○○
- ___ ○○○○○
- ___ ○○○○○
- ___ ○○○○○
- ___ ○○○○○

QUANTUM POOL
●●●●●●●●●●●●●●●●●●●●●●●●●○○○○○○○○○
□□□□□□□□□□□□□□□□□□□□□□□□□□□□□□□□□□

Hunter-Team Leader

Japan is not a place that accepts outsiders or the unusual. You came from a traditional, business-class family and had typical, business class aspirations for yourself. You were well on your way to achieving some limited success; you had a wife and child, and things looked, well, fine. Not exciting, not particularly promising, but fine. Then you erupted.

It happened on the job, sitting in front of your computer. Your eyes had been hurting for weeks, and now the pain had spread to the back of your head. Over-the-counter painkillers did nothing, and you were about ready to try something more potent when your mind exploded. All the tension, all the worries, all the pent-up rage burst forth. Unfortunately, they turned your cubicle-mate's brain to mush and knocked 14 others unconscious. No doubt about it, you were now a nova, and everyone knew it.

You did as you were expected to in those days. You reported to the government and Project Utopia for training and handling. Utopia paid you legal expenses and made sure you and your family suffered no repercussions from the damage (and the death) you caused. Although the death was tragic, your eruption as a nova of some ability made your family proud, especially your young son. Old friends, co-workers and casual acquaintances began to view you as a celebrity, even a hero. Of course, as of yet, you had done nothing to deserve such recognition.

Under Project Utopia's guidance, you mastered your mental abilities and tried to use them for good. However, the more you worked with Utopia, the more you came to realize that the United Nations' and Utopia's goals were not necessarily what was best for Japan and your family and friends. You soon came to resent the subtle, and not-so-subtle, ways Utopia was trying to influence you, use you to further its causes and support its policies. From the inside, you could see that the Project was not all its press claimed it was. When your son started talking about how perfect Team Tomorrow was, how he wanted to be just like them and move to Addis Ababa, that was the last straw.

You publicly cut all relations with Utopia and went on local and national networks discussing your reasons. You found that you had a lot of support from people who held similar fears, fears that Utopia was taking away Japan's newest resource, novas, and perverting them for its own schemes. Soon however, Utopia-sponsored critics drowned out your voice with their own platitudes and lies. Your friends stopped talking to you; your son was ashamed to be seen with you. Then the Directive came to you.

It offered you a new life, working for it and stopping novas that threatened Japan and the rest of the world. At first, you were skeptical of working for another international organization, but the Directive allayed your fears. Your superiors were Japanese, their interests were the good of Japan and its allies. Here you found a group where you could really belong and use your abilities as they were meant to be used: to help your people and your country.

Image: A Japanese man in your mid-30s, you're typically wearing the uniform of a Directive Blue and White.

Roleplaying Notes: You are a taciturn, very serious man. Your job, hunt down rogue and dangerous novas and capture or kill them. You rely on your mind, its offensive power and the superb intelligence the Directive supplies you. You always think things through before acting, making sure that you know all the angles, all the possible outcomes, and all your target's weaknesses before you strike. As for friends, well, you prefer respect and obedience to friendship and camaraderie. Although you work with others efficiently and effectively, you have no confidants or close ties within or outside of the Directive except your family.

Gear: Lock gun, nova restraints, flechette rifle

ABERRANT CHARACTER SHEET

Birth Name: Hunter-Team Leader
Code Name:
Series:

Eruption:
Nature: Bravo
Allegiance: Directive

ATTRIBUTES AND ABILITIES

PHYSICAL

STRENGTH ●●○○○
- Brawl ○○○○○
- Might ○○○○○
- ___ ○○○○○

DEXTERITY ●●●●●
- Athletics ○○○○○
- Drive ●●○○○
- Firearms ●●●○○
- Legerdemain ○○○○○
- MartialArts ●●○○○
- Melee ○○○○○
- Pilot ○○○○○
- Stealth ●●○○○
- ___ ○○○○○
- ___ ○○○○○

STAMINA ●●●●○
- Endurance ●●●○○
- Resistance ●●●○○
- ___ ○○○○○
- ___ ○○○○○

MENTAL

PERCEPTION ●●●○○
- Awareness ○○○○○
- Investigation ○○○○○
- ___ ○○○○○

INTELLIGENCE ●●●●●
- Analysis ○○○○○
- Bureaucracy ○○○○○
- Computer ○○○○○
- Engineering ○○○○○
- Intrusion ●●●○○
- Linguistics ○○○○○
- Medicine ○○○○○
- Science ○○○○○
- Survival ○○○○○
- Tradecraft ○○○○○

WITS ●●●●●
- Arts ○○○○○
- Rapport ○○○○○
- Shadowing ○○○○○
- Thought Discipline ●●○○○

SOCIAL

APPEARANCE ●●○○○
- Intimidation ●●●○○
- Style ○○○○○
- ___ ○○○○○

MANIPULATION ●●○○○
- Interrogation ○○○○○
- Streetwise ○○○○○
- Subterfuge ○○○○○
- ___ ○○○○○
- ___ ○○○○○
- ___ ○○○○○
- ___ ○○○○○

CHARISMA ●●○○○
- Command ○○○○○
- Etiquette ○○○○○
- Perform ○○○○○
- ___ ○○○○○
- ___ ○○○○○
- ___ ○○○○○
- ___ ○○○○○

ADVANTAGES

BACKGROUNDS
- Cipher ●●●○○
- Equipment ●●●●●
- Favors ●●●○○
- Resources ●●○○○
- ___ ○○○○○
- ___ ○○○○○

WILLPOWER
●●●●●●●○○○
☐☐☐☐☐☐☐☐☐☐

TAINT
○○○○○○○○○○
☐☐☐☐☐☐☐☐☐☐

ABERRATIONS
- ___
- ___
- ___

QUANTUM
●●●●○○○○○○

MEGA-ATTRIBUTES
- Mega-Wits ●○○○○
- (Enhanced Initiative)
- ___ ○○○○○
- ___ ○○○○○
- ___ ○○○○○
- ___ ○○○○○
- ___ ○○○○○
- ___ ○○○○○
- ___ ○○○○○
- ___ ○○○○○
- ___ ○○○○○

QUANTUM POWERS
- Mental Blast ●●●●○
- ___ ○○○○○
- ___ ○○○○○
- ___ ○○○○○
- ___ ○○○○○
- ___ ○○○○○
- ___ ○○○○○
- ___ ○○○○○
- ___ ○○○○○
- ___ ○○○○○

QUANTUM POOL
●●●●●●●●●●●●●●●●●●●●●●●●●●●○○○○○○
☐☐☐☐☐☐☐☐☐☐☐☐☐☐☐☐☐☐☐☐☐☐☐☐☐☐☐☐☐☐☐

CREDITS

Credits

Authors: Carl Bowen, Richard Dakan, Kyle Olson
Additional Material by: John Chambers
Developer: Kraig Blackwelder
Editor: John Chambers
Art Director: Rich Thomas
Artists: Mike Danze, Talon Dunning, Steve Ellis, Langdon Foss
Cover Artist: Michael Gaydos
Cover Design: Brian Glass
Layout, Typesetting and Design: Brian Glass

735 PARK NORTH BLVD.
SUITE 128
CLARKSTON, GA 30021
USA

TABLE OF CONTENTS